Now, this is very important: Mom and I had 3 special newcomers join our lives this past year:

The cat

THE CAT [Felinus snoozus]:
A more-or-less vertebrate animal that mostly inhabits laundry baskets. The deal is simple: we give him food and shelter, and in exchange, he does nothing.
(well, sometimes he scratches us)

UNEDITED PHOTO. HE'S NOT A PRETTY SIGHT WHEN HE FIRST WAKES UP...

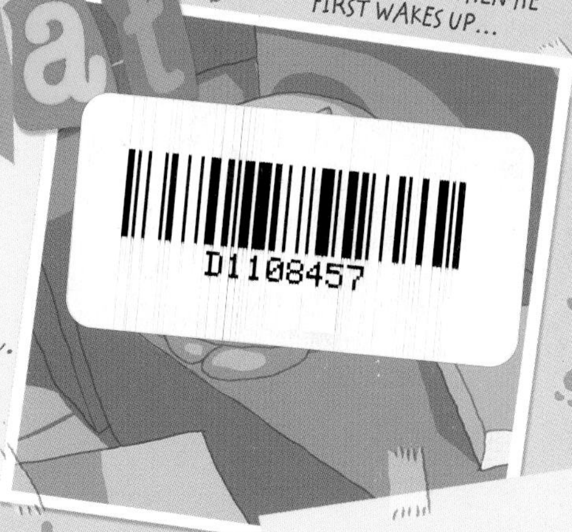

We change the cat's name every week. Recently, he's been called:

- DOM PERIGNON
- BUNNY
- CHOCO
- BASIL FAWLTY
- SHNOOKUMS
- INKSPOT
- AIRHEAD
- THE MAxxx
- JAWS

HOW COULD I POSSIBLY BE NORMAL?

The neighbor, a.k.a. "THE MAN IN THE DEAD SHEEP VEST" ...as I call him

NOOOO, MERCY!

Richard

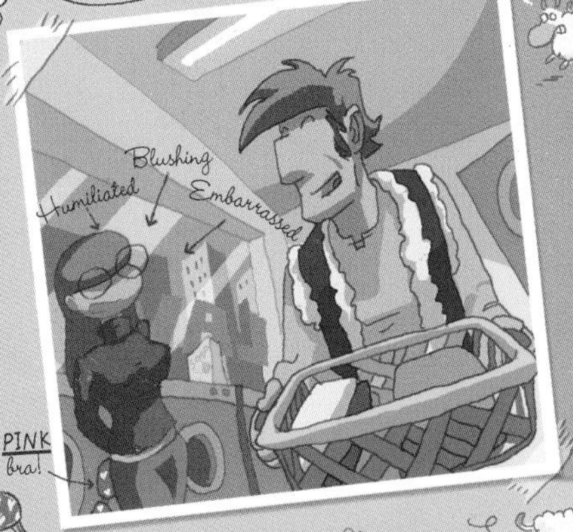

Blushing
Humiliated
Embarrassed

PINK bra!

w/ li'l hearts (WHOHOOO!)

When he moved into the building, I saw right away that there could be something between him and Mom. And of course, it was love at first sight. But it's still not official yet: whenever they meet, they babble like dodoes and turn bright red...

Tristan

Not really a first meeting. I used to watch him through the window, in the building across the street, ever since I was little. But I finally worked up the courage to talk to him... And we became "just friends"... And then one day, I decided to tell him how I really feel... To sum it up: when I got there, his apartment was empty. Poof. Gone. Without a word. Nothing.

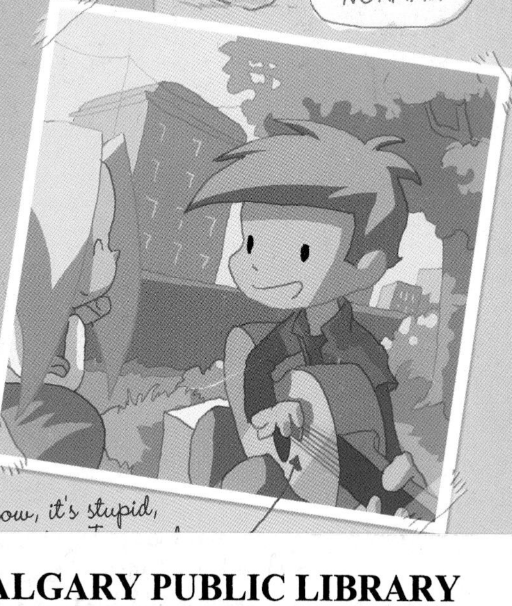

Fender

I know, it's stupid,

SO EMBARRASSED

Lou! ②

Summertime Blues

JULIEN NEEL

GRAPHIC UNIVERSE™ · MINNEAPOLIS · NEW YORK

TO MY MOM

Story and art by Julien Neel

Translation by Carol Klio Burrell

First American edition published in 2012 by Graphic Universe™.

Lou! by Julien Neel © 2004 — Glénat Editions
© 2012 Lerner Publishing Group, Inc. for the US edition

Graphic Universe™ is a trademark of Lerner Publishing Group, Inc.

Graphic Universe™
A division of Lerner Publishing Group, Inc.
241 First Avenue North
Minneapolis, MN 55401 U.S.A.

Website address: www.lernerbooks.com

Library of Congress Cataloging-in-Publication Data

Neel, Julien.
    [Mortebouse. English]
    Summertime blues / by Julien Neel ; illustrated by Julien Neel ; translation by Carol Klio Burrell.
        p.   cm. — (Lou! ; #2)
    Summary: Twelve–year–old Lou's attempt to play matchmaker for her mother and Richard are foiled by a mandatory visit with her grandmother, which is marked by boredom, Brussels sprouts, and Memaw's own plans for Mom's love life.
    ISBN: 978–0–7613–8777–0 (lib. bdg. : alk. paper)
    1. Graphic novels [1. Graphic novels 2. Grandmothers—Fiction. 3. Mothers and daughters—Fiction. 4. Dating (Social customs)—Fiction.] I. Burrell, Carol Klio. II. Title.
PZ7.7.N44Su 2012
741.5'944—dc23   2011037042

Manufactured in the United States of America
1 – BC – 12/31/11

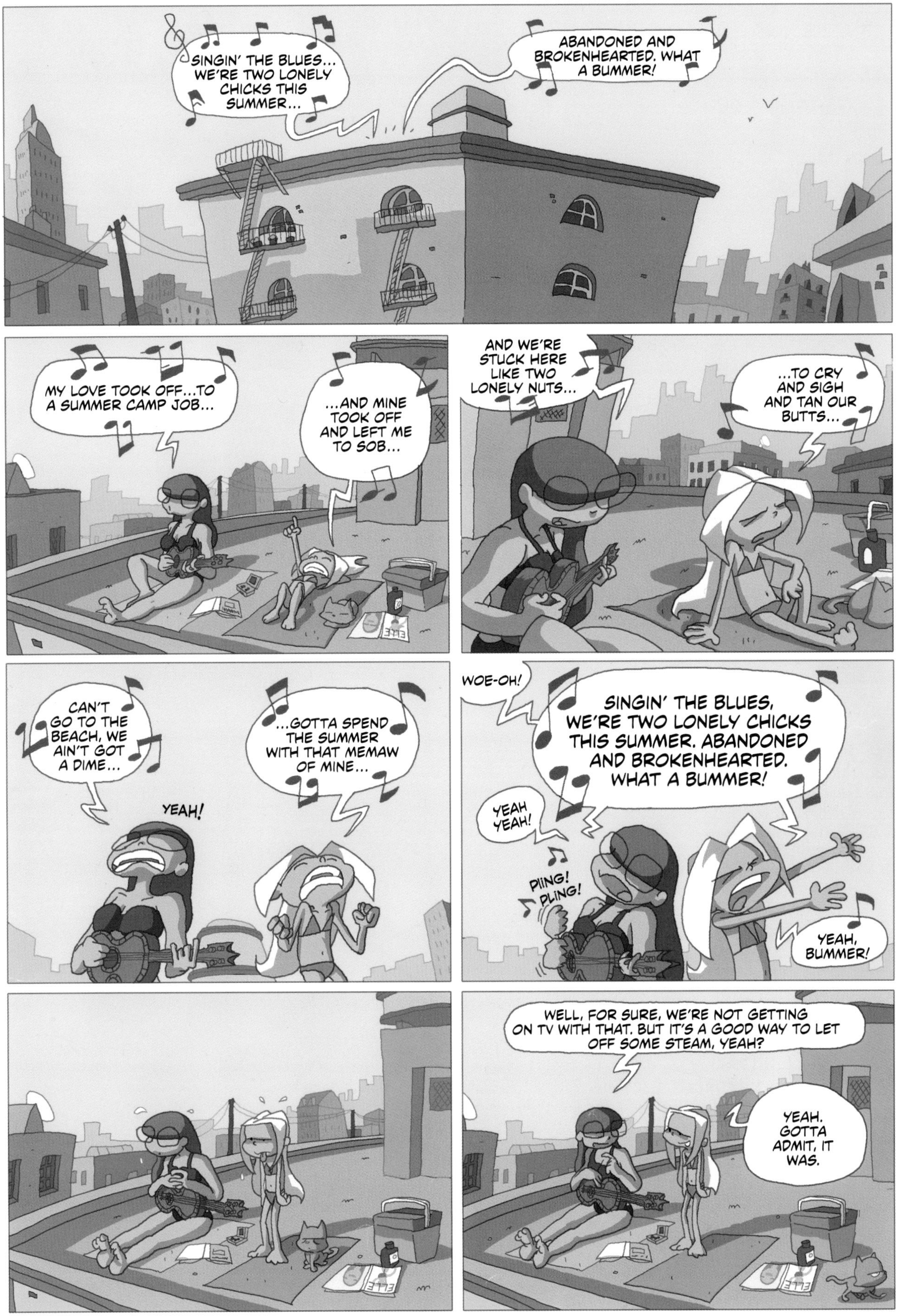
SINGIN' THE BLUES... WE'RE TWO LONELY CHICKS THIS SUMMER...
ABANDONED AND BROKENHEARTED. WHAT A BUMMER!
MY LOVE TOOK OFF...TO A SUMMER CAMP JOB...
...AND MINE TOOK OFF AND LEFT ME TO SOB...
AND WE'RE STUCK HERE LIKE TWO LONELY NUTS...
...TO CRY AND SIGH AND TAN OUR BUTTS...
CAN'T GO TO THE BEACH, WE AIN'T GOT A DIME...
YEAH!
...GOTTA SPEND THE SUMMER WITH THAT MEMAW OF MINE...
WOE-OH!
SINGIN' THE BLUES, WE'RE TWO LONELY CHICKS THIS SUMMER. ABANDONED AND BROKENHEARTED. WHAT A BUMMER!
YEAH YEAH!
PLING! PLING!
YEAH, BUMMER!
WELL, FOR SURE, WE'RE NOT GETTING ON TV WITH THAT. BUT IT'S A GOOD WAY TO LET OFF SOME STEAM, YEAH?
YEAH. GOTTA ADMIT, IT WAS.

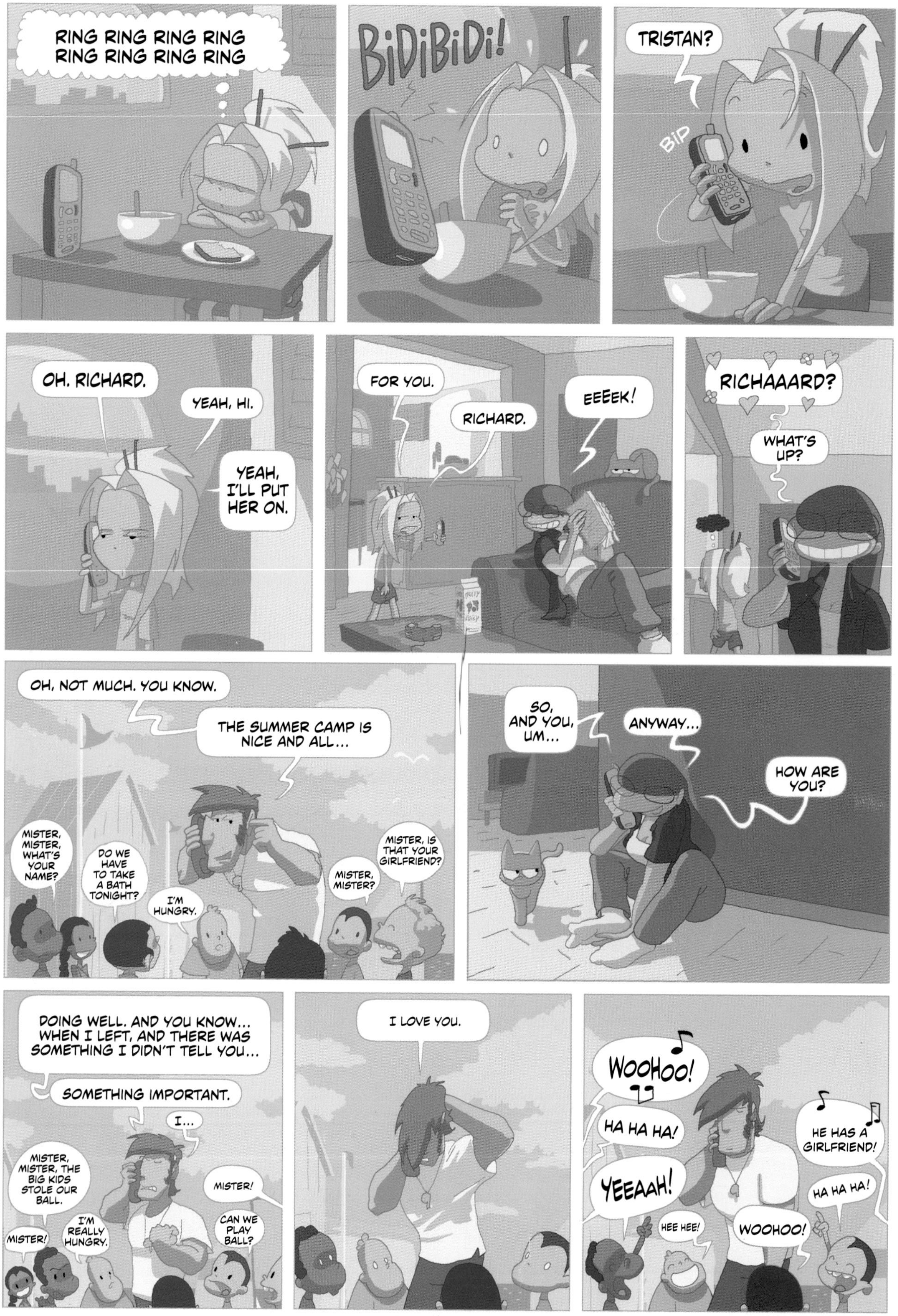
RING RING RING RING
RING RING RING RING
BiDiBiDi!
TRISTAN?
BiP
OH. RICHARD.
YEAH, HI.
YEAH, I'LL PUT HER ON.
FOR YOU.
RICHARD.
EEEEK!
RICHAAARD?
WHAT'S UP?
OH, NOT MUCH. YOU KNOW.
THE SUMMER CAMP IS NICE AND ALL...
MISTER, MISTER, WHAT'S YOUR NAME?
DO WE HAVE TO TAKE A BATH TONIGHT?
I'M HUNGRY.
MISTER, MISTER?
MISTER, IS THAT YOUR GIRLFRIEND?
SO, AND YOU, UM...
ANYWAY...
HOW ARE YOU?
DOING WELL. AND YOU KNOW... WHEN I LEFT, AND THERE WAS SOMETHING I DIDN'T TELL YOU...
SOMETHING IMPORTANT.
I...
MISTER, MISTER, THE BIG KIDS STOLE OUR BALL.
MISTER!
I'M REALLY HUNGRY.
MISTER!
CAN WE PLAY BALL?
I LOVE YOU.
WOOHOO!
HA HA HA!
YEEAAH!
HEE HEE!
WOOHOO!
HE HAS A GIRLFRIEND!
HA HA HA!

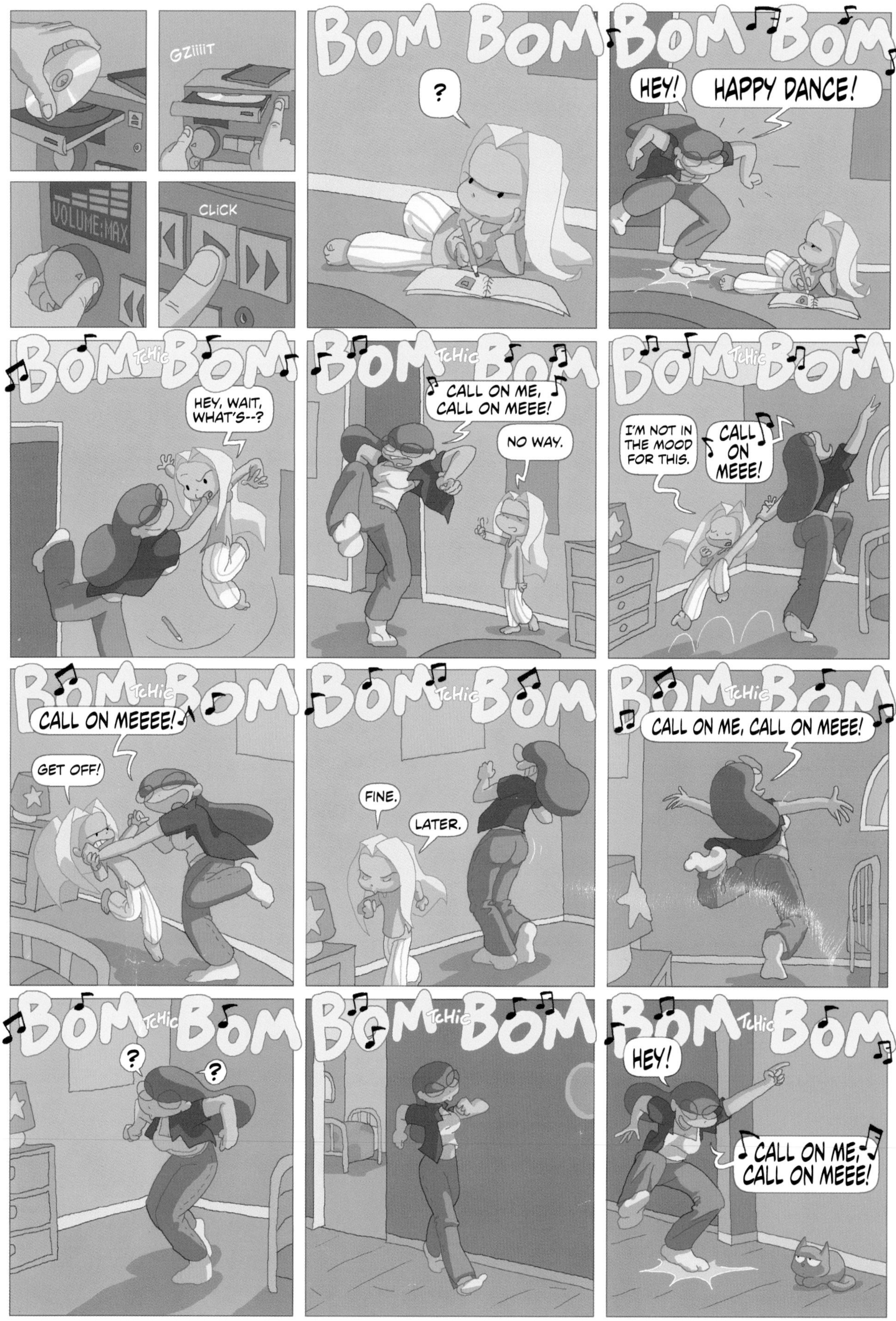
GZiiiiT
CLiCK
VOLUME:MAX
BOM BOM BOM BOM
?
HEY!
HAPPY DANCE!
BOM TCHIC BOM
HEY, WAIT, WHAT'S--?
BOM TCHIC BOM
CALL ON ME, CALL ON MEEE!
NO WAY.
BOM TCHIC BOM
I'M NOT IN THE MOOD FOR THIS.
CALL ON MEEE!
BOM TCHIC BOM
CALL ON MEEEE!
GET OFF!
BOM TCHIC BOM
FINE.
LATER.
BOM TCHIC BOM
CALL ON ME, CALL ON MEEE!
BOM TCHIC BOM
?
?
BOM TCHIC BOM
BOM TCHIC BOM
HEY!
CALL ON ME, CALL ON MEEE!

SO ANYWAY...HAVE A GOOD VACATION...

SURE...YOU TOO...

HMPH! EASY FOR YOU TO SAY. SPENDING THE SUMMER WITH MY GRANDMOTHER? YOU HAVE NO IDEA.

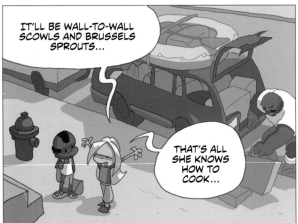

IT'LL BE WALL-TO-WALL SCOWLS AND BRUSSELS SPROUTS...

THAT'S ALL SHE KNOWS HOW TO COOK...

AND EVERY TIME MEMAW AND MOM LOOK AT EACH OTHER, THEY ARGUE.

BAH. AT LEAST IT'S OUT IN THE COUNTRY...

THE COUNTRY IS PRETTY...

PRETTY? A MUDDY VILLAGE FULL OF STUPID ANIMALS?

WHOA, CALM DOWN!

PEACE!

SORRY. BUT I'M TELLING YOU, IT'S THE END OF THE WORLD, DOWN THERE.

AREN'T YOU EXAGGERATING JUST A LITTLE?

EVEN THE FLOWERS SMELL LIKE POO. THE MOSQUITOES ARE AS BIG AS MY FIST...IT'S SO HUMID THAT IF YOU DON'T KEEP MOVING, YOU SINK INTO THE MUD...BUT...THAT'S NOT THE WORST!

UH... WHAT'S THE WORST?

MY CELL PHONE WON'T WORK THERE!

NOOOO?

OH YEAH. THAT'S THE END OF THE WORLD.

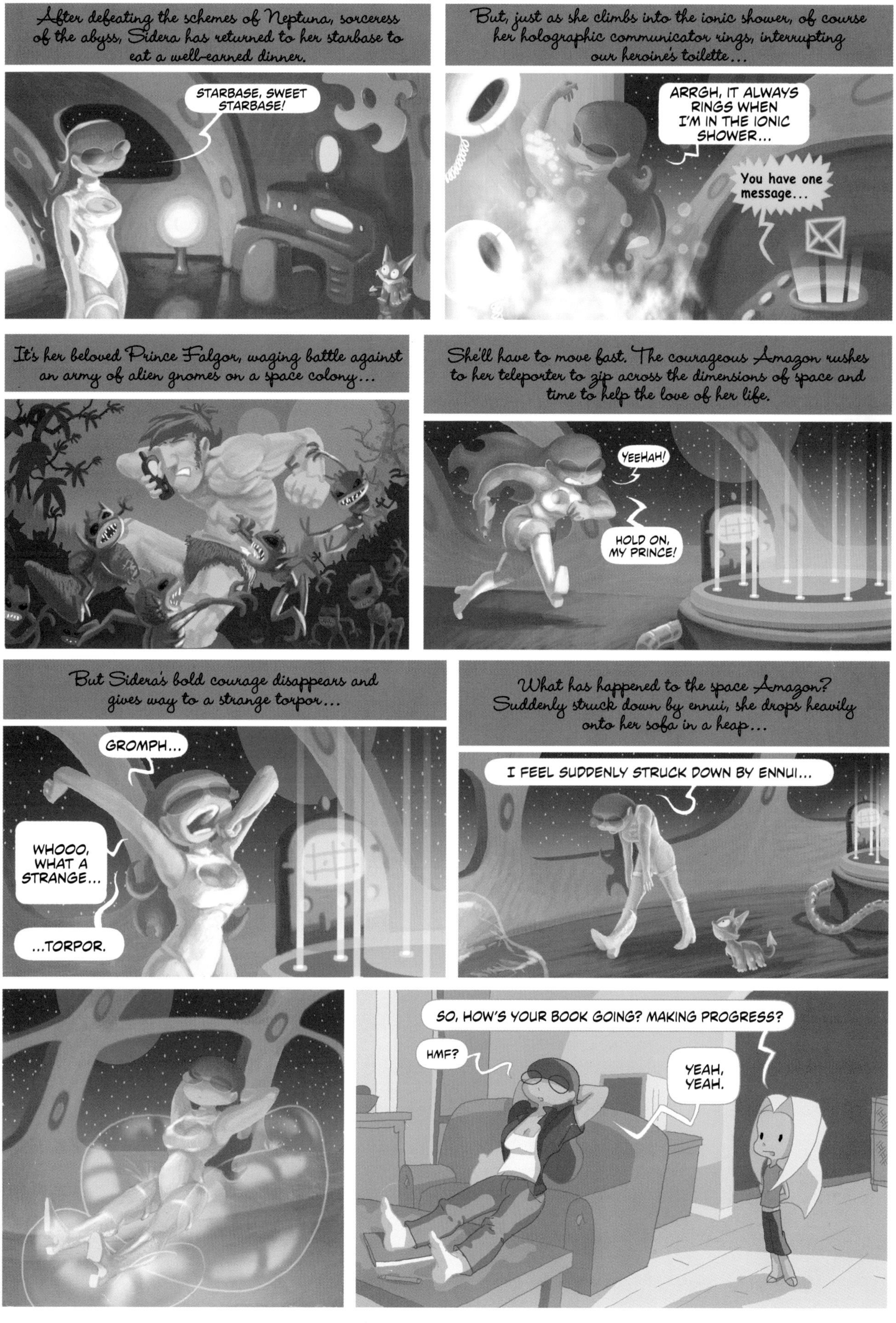
After defeating the schemes of Neptuna, sorceress of the abyss, Sidera has returned to her starbase to eat a well-earned dinner.
STARBASE, SWEET STARBASE!
But, just as she climbs into the ionic shower, of course her holographic communicator rings, interrupting our heroine's toilette...
ARRGH, IT ALWAYS RINGS WHEN I'M IN THE IONIC SHOWER...
You have one message...
It's her beloved Prince Falgor, waging battle against an army of alien gnomes on a space colony...
She'll have to move fast. The courageous Amazon rushes to her teleporter to zip across the dimensions of space and time to help the love of her life.
YEEHAH!
HOLD ON, MY PRINCE!
But Sidera's bold courage disappears and gives way to a strange torpor...
GROMPH...
WHOOO, WHAT A STRANGE...
...TORPOR.
What has happened to the space Amazon? Suddenly struck down by ennui, she drops heavily onto her sofa in a heap...
I FEEL SUDDENLY STRUCK DOWN BY ENNUI...
SO, HOW'S YOUR BOOK GOING? MAKING PROGRESS?
HMF?
YEAH, YEAH.

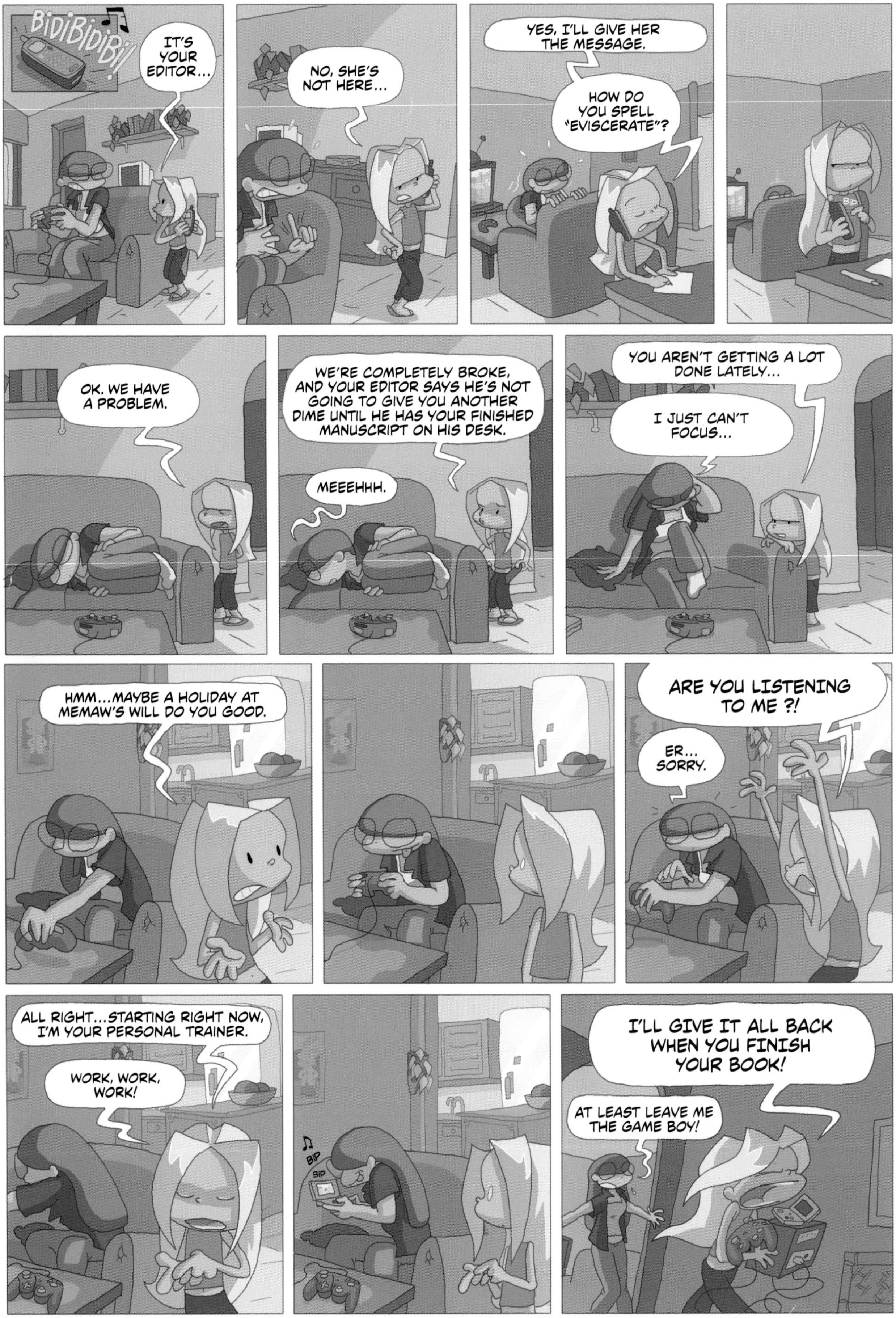
BIDIBIDIBI!
IT'S YOUR EDITOR...
NO, SHE'S NOT HERE...
YES, I'LL GIVE HER THE MESSAGE.
HOW DO YOU SPELL "EVISCERATE"?
BIP
OK. WE HAVE A PROBLEM.
WE'RE COMPLETELY BROKE, AND YOUR EDITOR SAYS HE'S NOT GOING TO GIVE YOU ANOTHER DIME UNTIL HE HAS YOUR FINISHED MANUSCRIPT ON HIS DESK.
MEEEHHH.
YOU AREN'T GETTING A LOT DONE LATELY...
I JUST CAN'T FOCUS...
HMM...MAYBE A HOLIDAY AT MEMAW'S WILL DO YOU GOOD.
ARE YOU LISTENING TO ME ?!
ER... SORRY.
ALL RIGHT...STARTING RIGHT NOW, I'M YOUR PERSONAL TRAINER.
WORK, WORK, WORK!
BIP
BIP
I'LL GIVE IT ALL BACK WHEN YOU FINISH YOUR BOOK!
AT LEAST LEAVE ME THE GAME BOY!

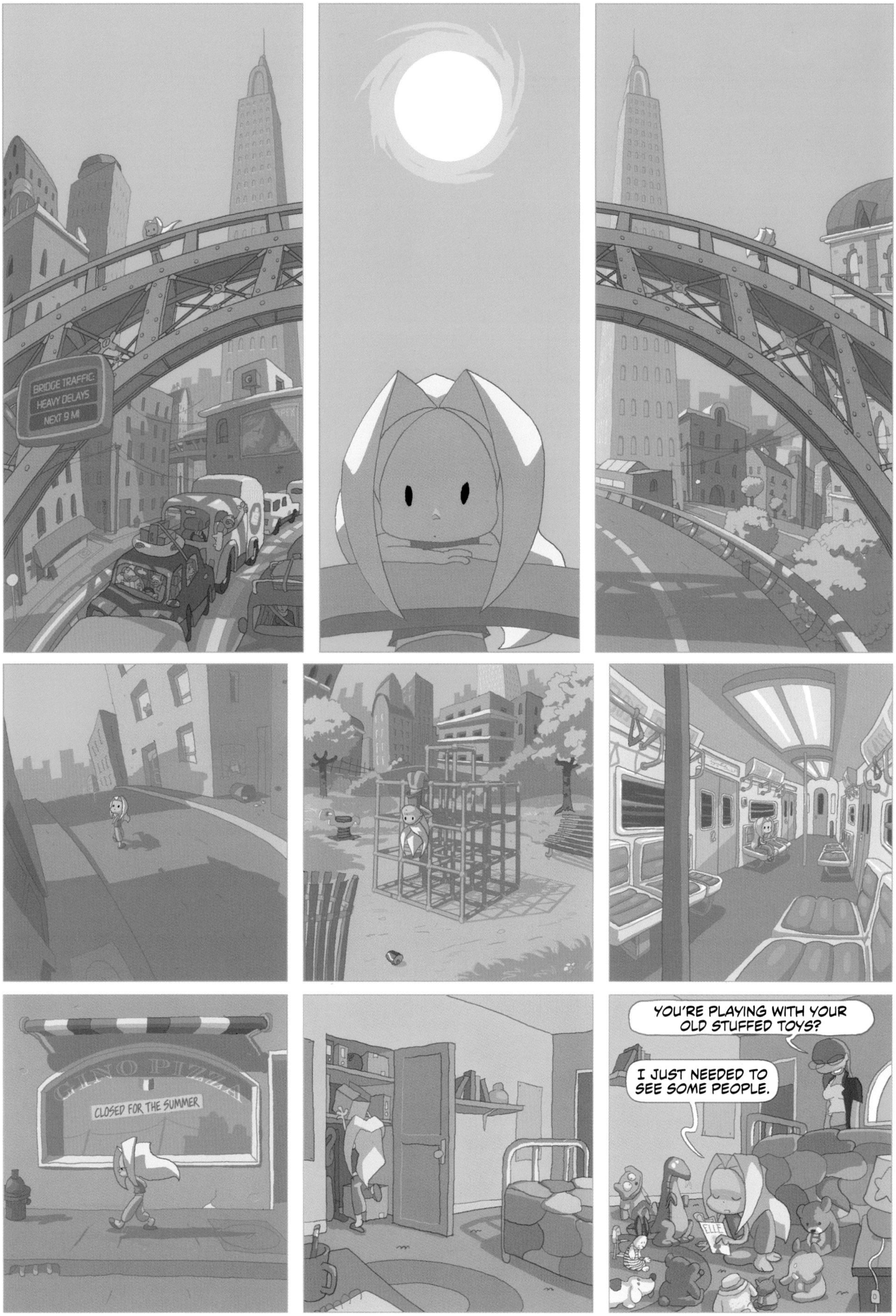
BRIDGE TRAFFIC:
HEAVY DELAYS
NEXT 9 MI
GINO PIZZA
CLOSED FOR THE SUMMER
YOU'RE PLAYING WITH YOUR OLD STUFFED TOYS?
I JUST NEEDED TO SEE SOME PEOPLE.

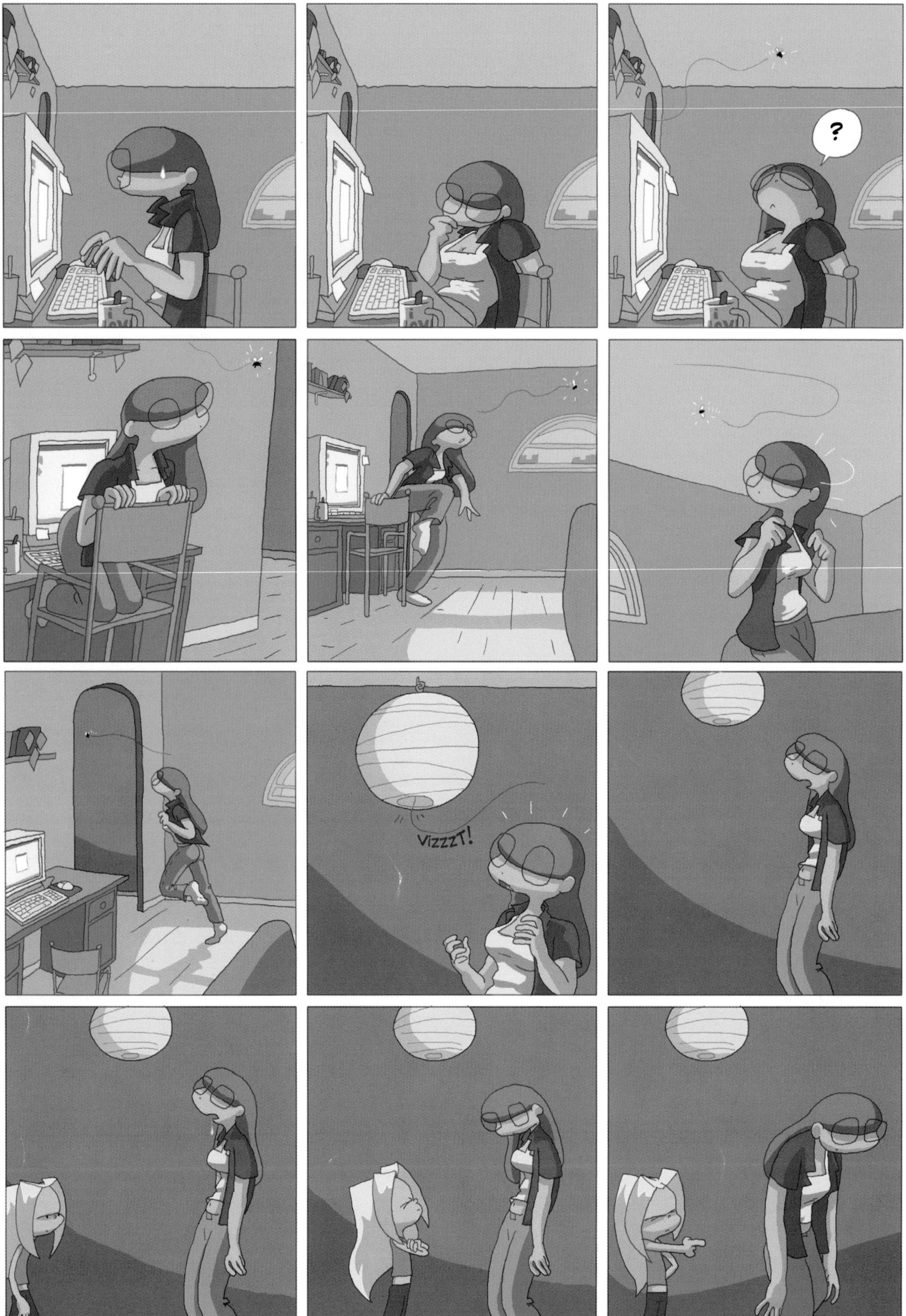
?
VIZZZT!

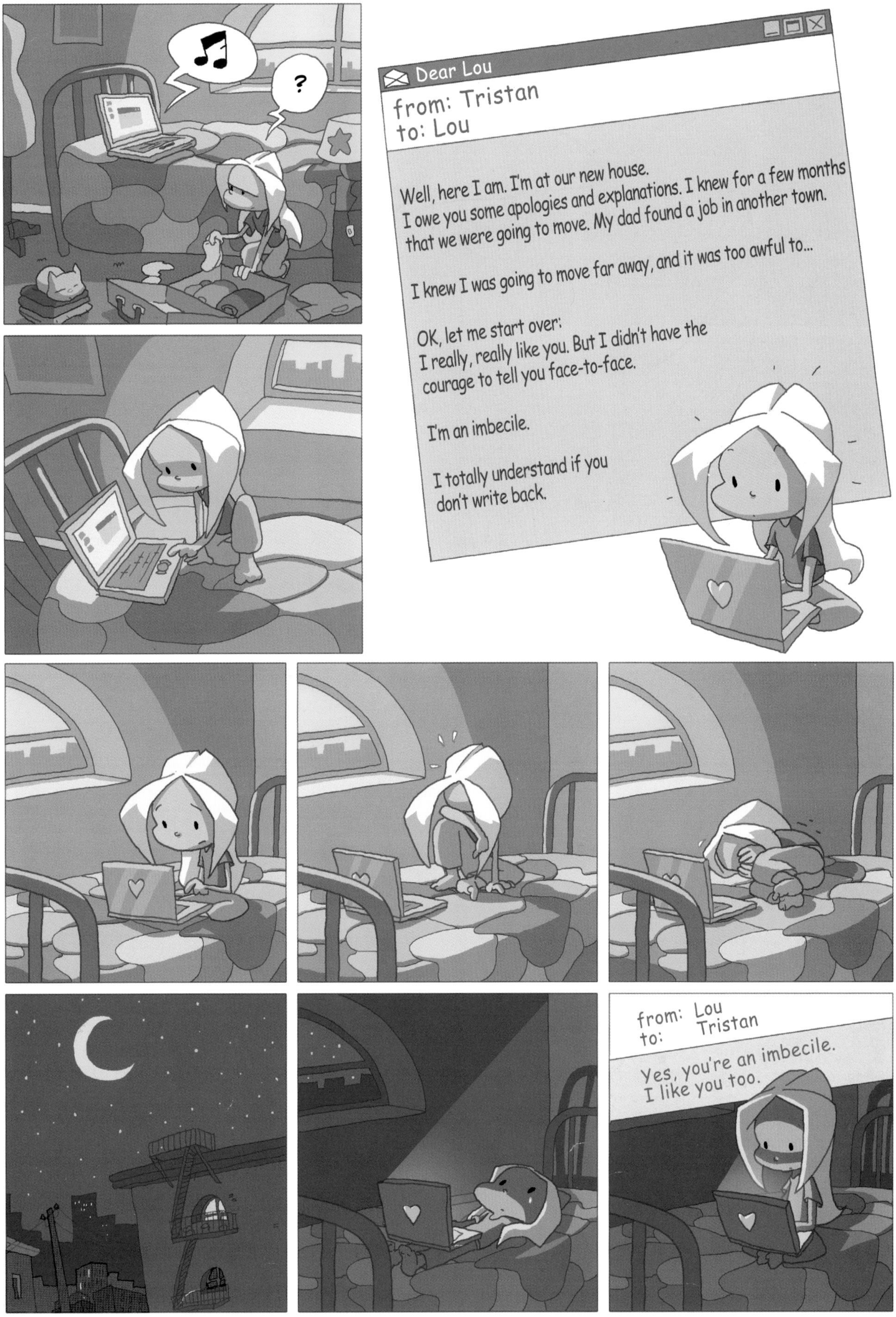
?
Dear Lou
from: Tristan
to: Lou
Well, here I am. I'm at our new house.
I owe you some apologies and explanations. I knew for a few months that we were going to move. My dad found a job in another town.
I knew I was going to move far away, and it was too awful to...
OK, let me start over:
I really, really like you. But I didn't have the courage to tell you face-to-face.
I'm an imbecile.
I totally understand if you don't write back.
from: Lou
to: Tristan
Yes, you're an imbecile.
I like you too.

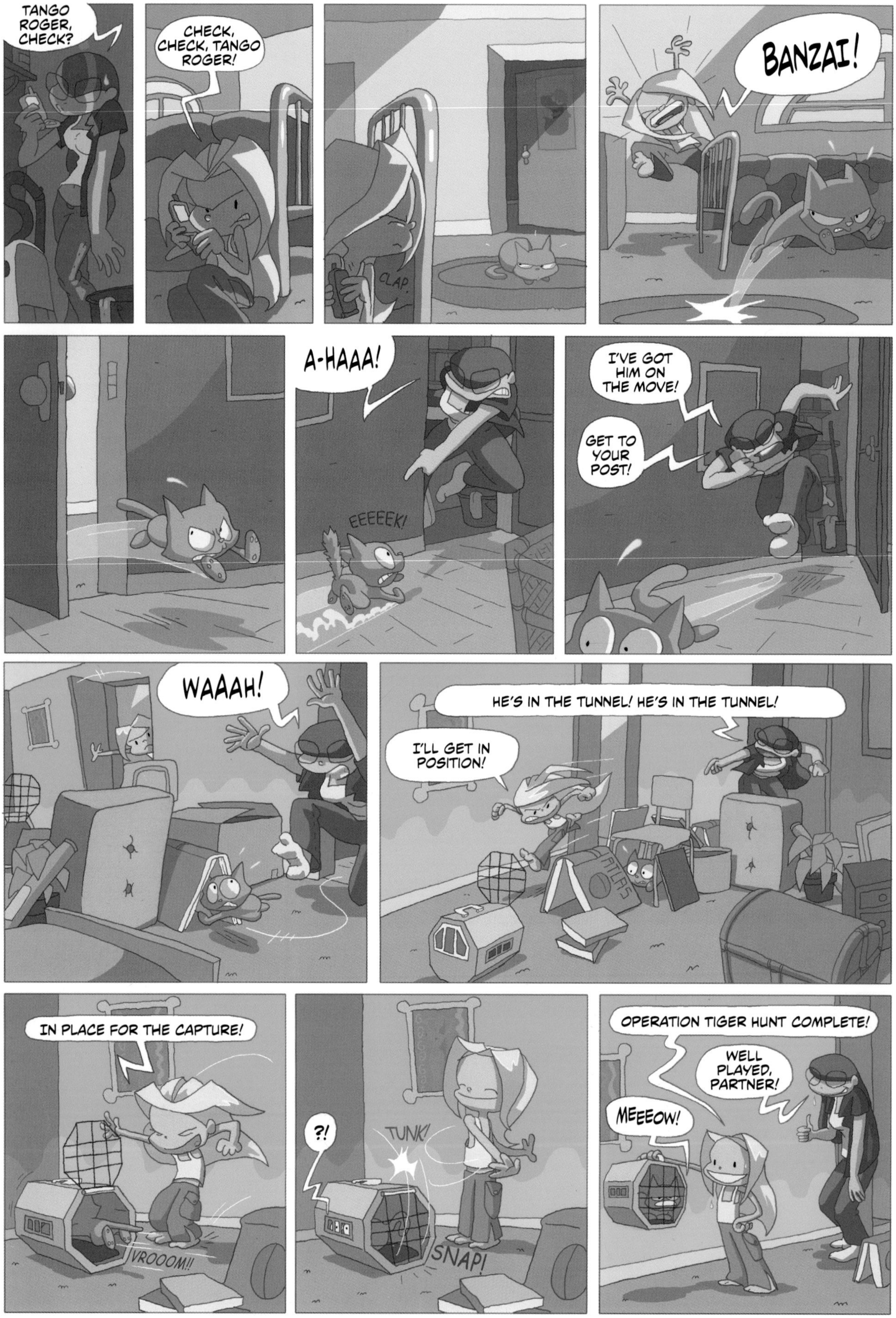
TANGO ROGER, CHECK?
CHECK, CHECK, TANGO ROGER!
CLAP.
BANZAI!
A-HAAA!
EEEEEK!
I'VE GOT HIM ON THE MOVE!
GET TO YOUR POST!
WAAAH!
HE'S IN THE TUNNEL! HE'S IN THE TUNNEL!
I'LL GET IN POSITION!
IN PLACE FOR THE CAPTURE!
VROOOM!!
?!
TUNK!
SNAP!
OPERATION TIGER HUNT COMPLETE!
WELL PLAYED, PARTNER!
MEEEOW!

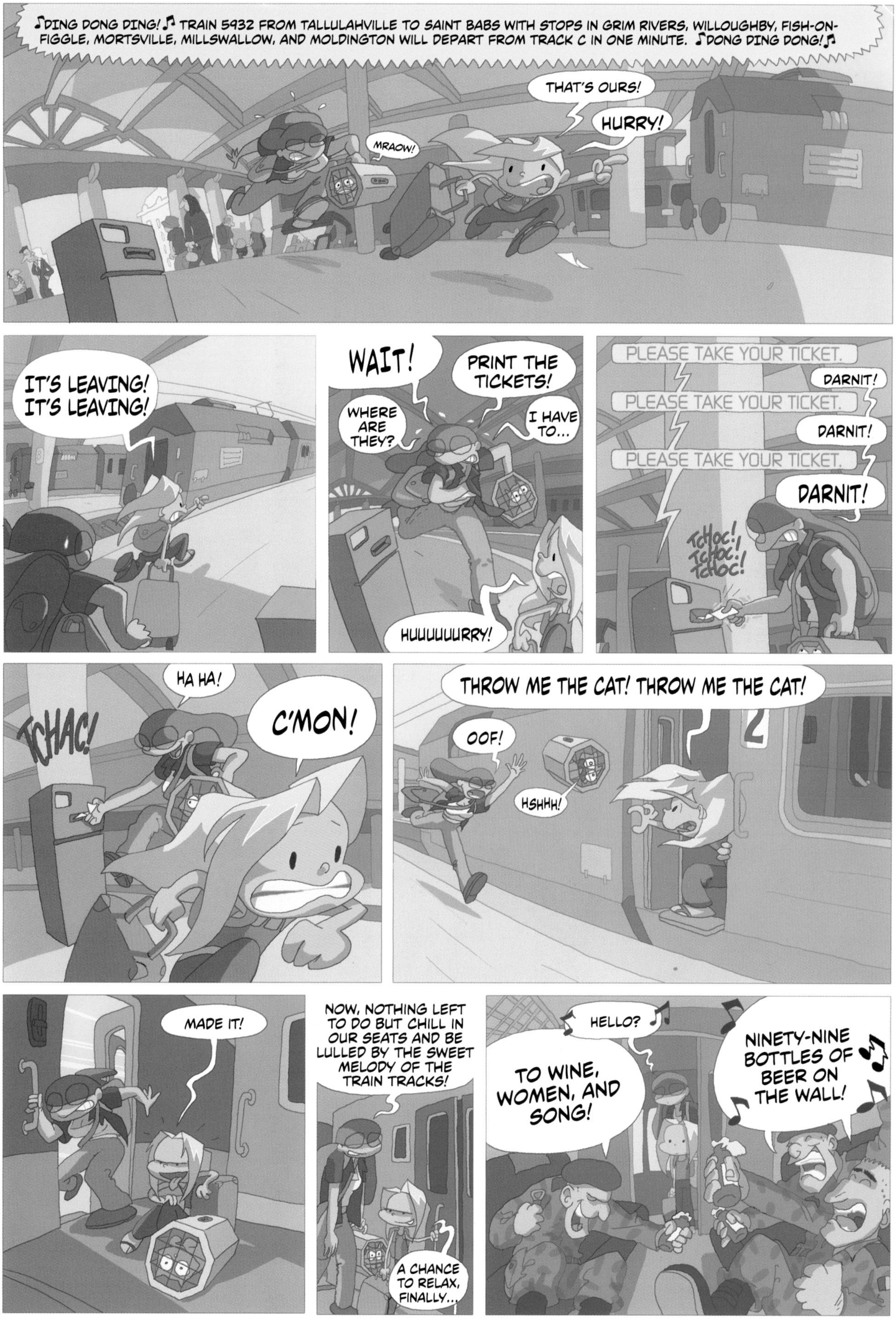
♪DING DONG DING! ♫ TRAIN 5932 FROM TALLULAHVILLE TO SAINT BABS WITH STOPS IN GRIM RIVERS, WILLOUGHBY, FISH-ON-FIGGLE, MORTSVILLE, MILLSWALLOW, AND MOLDINGTON WILL DEPART FROM TRACK C IN ONE MINUTE. ♪DONG DING DONG!♫
THAT'S OURS!
HURRY!
MRAOW!
IT'S LEAVING! IT'S LEAVING!
WAIT!
PRINT THE TICKETS!
WHERE ARE THEY?
I HAVE TO...
HUUUUUURRY!
PLEASE TAKE YOUR TICKET.
DARNIT!
PLEASE TAKE YOUR TICKET.
DARNIT!
PLEASE TAKE YOUR TICKET.
DARNIT!
TCHOC! TCHOC! TCHOC!
HA HA!
TCHAC!
C'MON!
THROW ME THE CAT! THROW ME THE CAT!
OOF!
HSHHH!
MADE IT!
NOW, NOTHING LEFT TO DO BUT CHILL IN OUR SEATS AND BE LULLED BY THE SWEET MELODY OF THE TRAIN TRACKS!
A CHANCE TO RELAX, FINALLY...
HELLO?
TO WINE, WOMEN, AND SONG!
NINETY-NINE BOTTLES OF BEER ON THE WALL!

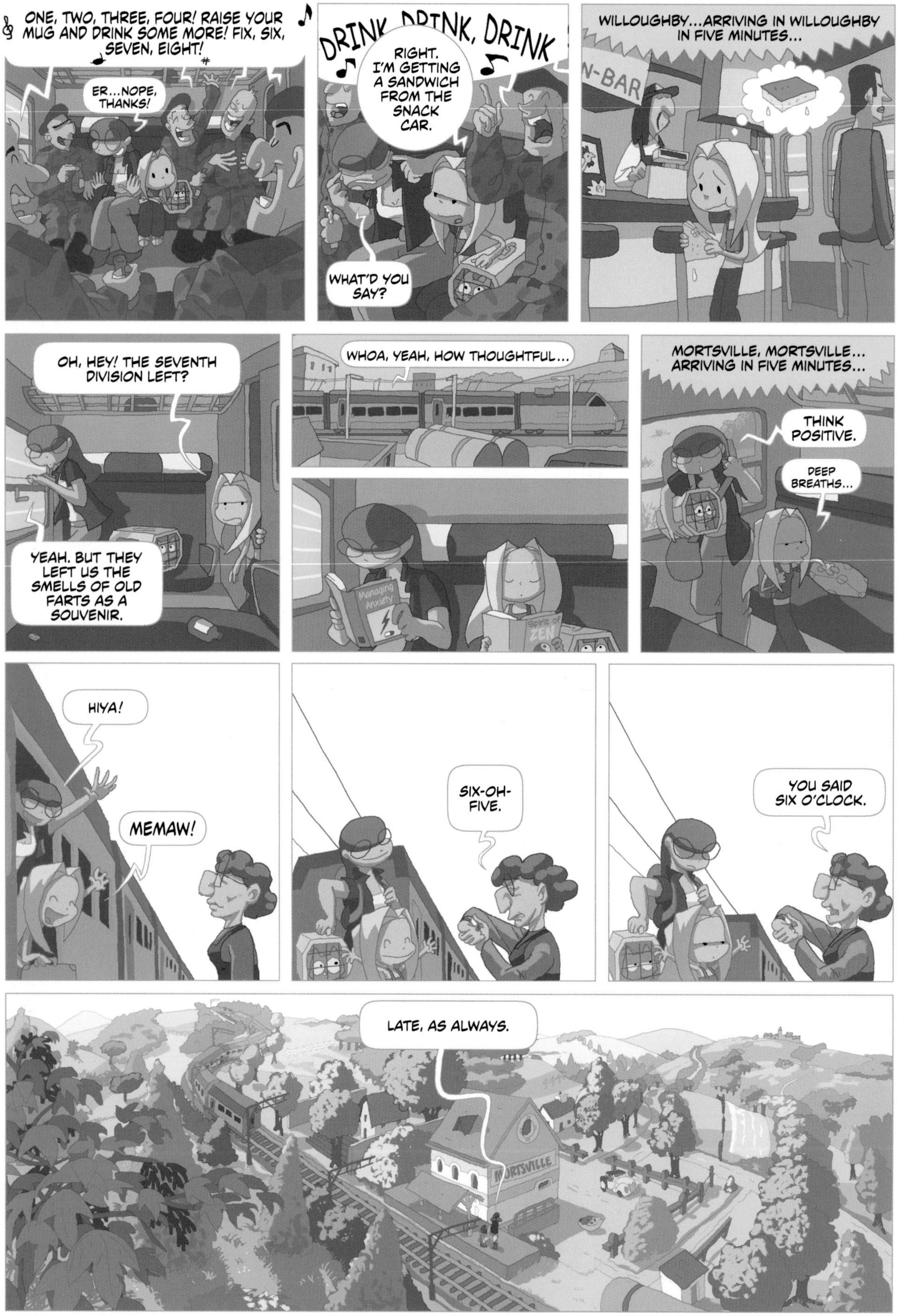
ONE, TWO, THREE, FOUR! RAISE YOUR MUG AND DRINK SOME MORE! FIX, SIX, SEVEN, EIGHT!
ER...NOPE, THANKS!
DRINK, DRINK, DRINK
RIGHT. I'M GETTING A SANDWICH FROM THE SNACK CAR.
WHAT'D YOU SAY?
WILLOUGHBY...ARRIVING IN WILLOUGHBY IN FIVE MINUTES...
N-BAR
OH, HEY! THE SEVENTH DIVISION LEFT?
YEAH. BUT THEY LEFT US THE SMELLS OF OLD FARTS AS A SOUVENIR.
WHOA, YEAH, HOW THOUGHTFUL...
Managing Anxiety
Spirit of ZEN
MORTSVILLE, MORTSVILLE... ARRIVING IN FIVE MINUTES...
THINK POSITIVE.
DEEP BREATHS...
HIYA!
MEMAW!
SIX-OH-FIVE.
YOU SAID SIX O'CLOCK.
LATE, AS ALWAYS.
MORTSVILLE

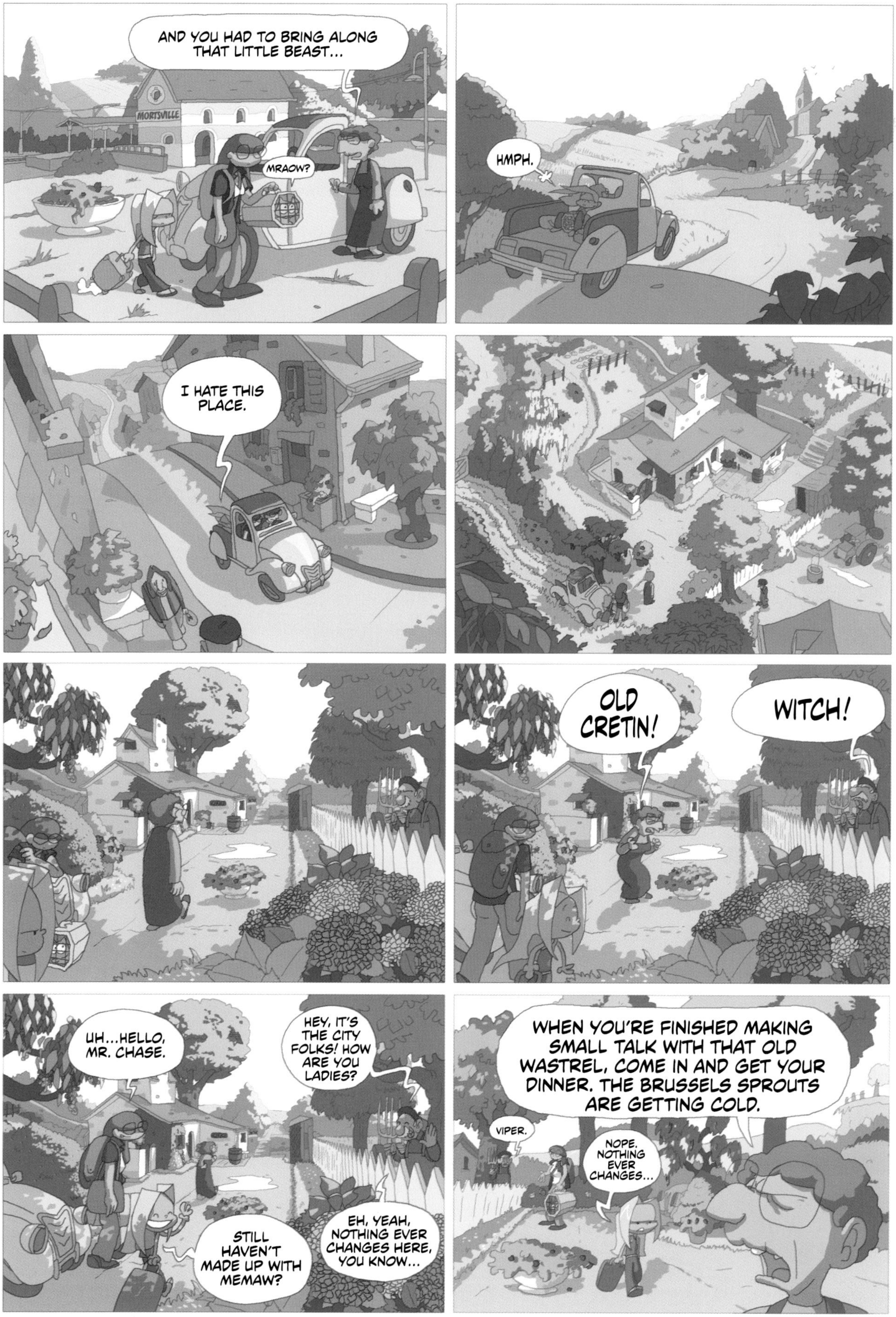
AND YOU HAD TO BRING ALONG THAT LITTLE BEAST...
MORTSVILLE
MRAOW?
HMPH.
I HATE THIS PLACE.
OLD CRETIN!
WITCH!
UH...HELLO, MR. CHASE.
HEY, IT'S THE CITY FOLKS! HOW ARE YOU LADIES?
STILL HAVEN'T MADE UP WITH MEMAW?
EH, YEAH, NOTHING EVER CHANGES HERE, YOU KNOW...
WHEN YOU'RE FINISHED MAKING SMALL TALK WITH THAT OLD WASTREL, COME IN AND GET YOUR DINNER. THE BRUSSELS SPROUTS ARE GETTING COLD.
VIPER.
NOPE. NOTHING EVER CHANGES...

C'MON, COME OUT. YOU CAN RUN AROUND!

OH, RIGHT! YOU DON'T KNOW ABOUT THAT. IT'S CALLED MUD.

THERE'S LOTS HERE.

FLITCH!

I'D LOVE TO SAY THAT YOU'LL GET USED TO IT AFTER A WHILE...

BUT THAT WOULDN'T BE TRUE.

THAT'S A FLOWER. F-L-O-W-E-R.

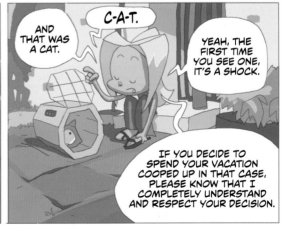

AND THAT WAS A CAT.

C-A-T.

YEAH, THE FIRST TIME YOU SEE ONE, IT'S A SHOCK.

IF YOU DECIDE TO SPEND YOUR VACATION COOPED UP IN THAT CASE, PLEASE KNOW THAT I COMPLETELY UNDERSTAND AND RESPECT YOUR DECISION.

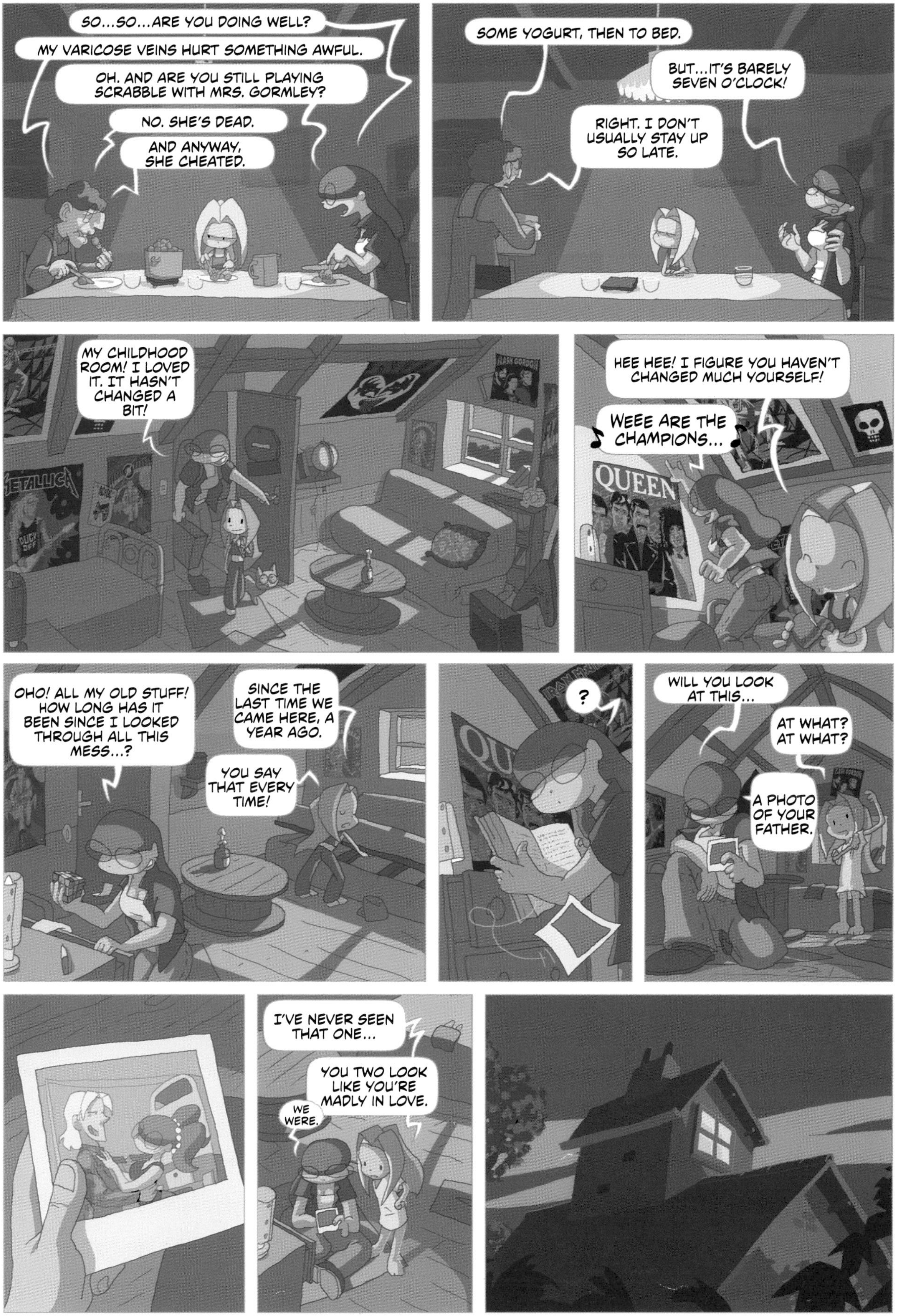
SO...SO...ARE YOU DOING WELL?
MY VARICOSE VEINS HURT SOMETHING AWFUL.
OH. AND ARE YOU STILL PLAYING SCRABBLE WITH MRS. GORMLEY?
NO. SHE'S DEAD.
AND ANYWAY, SHE CHEATED.
SOME YOGURT, THEN TO BED.
BUT...IT'S BARELY SEVEN O'CLOCK!
RIGHT. I DON'T USUALLY STAY UP SO LATE.
MY CHILDHOOD ROOM! I LOVED IT. IT HASN'T CHANGED A BIT!
HEE HEE! I FIGURE YOU HAVEN'T CHANGED MUCH YOURSELF!
WEEE ARE THE CHAMPIONS...
QUEEN
OHO! ALL MY OLD STUFF! HOW LONG HAS IT BEEN SINCE I LOOKED THROUGH ALL THIS MESS...?
SINCE THE LAST TIME WE CAME HERE, A YEAR AGO.
YOU SAY THAT EVERY TIME!
?
WILL YOU LOOK AT THIS...
AT WHAT? AT WHAT?
A PHOTO OF YOUR FATHER.
I'VE NEVER SEEN THAT ONE...
YOU TWO LOOK LIKE YOU'RE MADLY IN LOVE.
WE WERE.

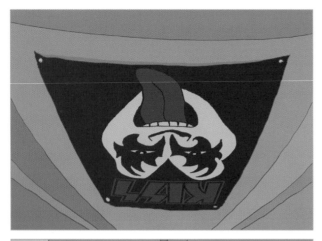

YOU DON'T HAVE THE RIGHT TO JUDGE MY LIFE!

I'M YOUR MOTHER, MAY I REMIND YOU!

SO SELF-CENTERED!

AAAAND... THEY'RE OFF!

WHY DON'T YOU SHOW ME SOME SUPPORT INSTEAD OF CRITICIZING EVERYTHING I DO!

MORNING!

DO YOU EXPECT ME TO ENCOURAGE YOU TO WASTE YOUR TIME SCRIBBLING THAT SCIENTOLOGY STUFF?

SCIENCE FICTION! MY NOVELS ARE SCIENCE FICTION!

SPACE EPIC, TO BE PRECISE.

PFFT. IDIOTIC!

I TOLD YOU! I FOUND YOU A FINE JOB AT THE VILLAGE POST OFFICE!

I WONDER IF ISAAC ASIMOV'S MOTHER WAS LIKE THIS...

RIGHTY-O, I'M GOING OUT...

SOMETHING I NEED TO SEE OUTSIDE.

PLANTS, ANIMALS, NATURE...

...THE WEATHER...

TAP TAP

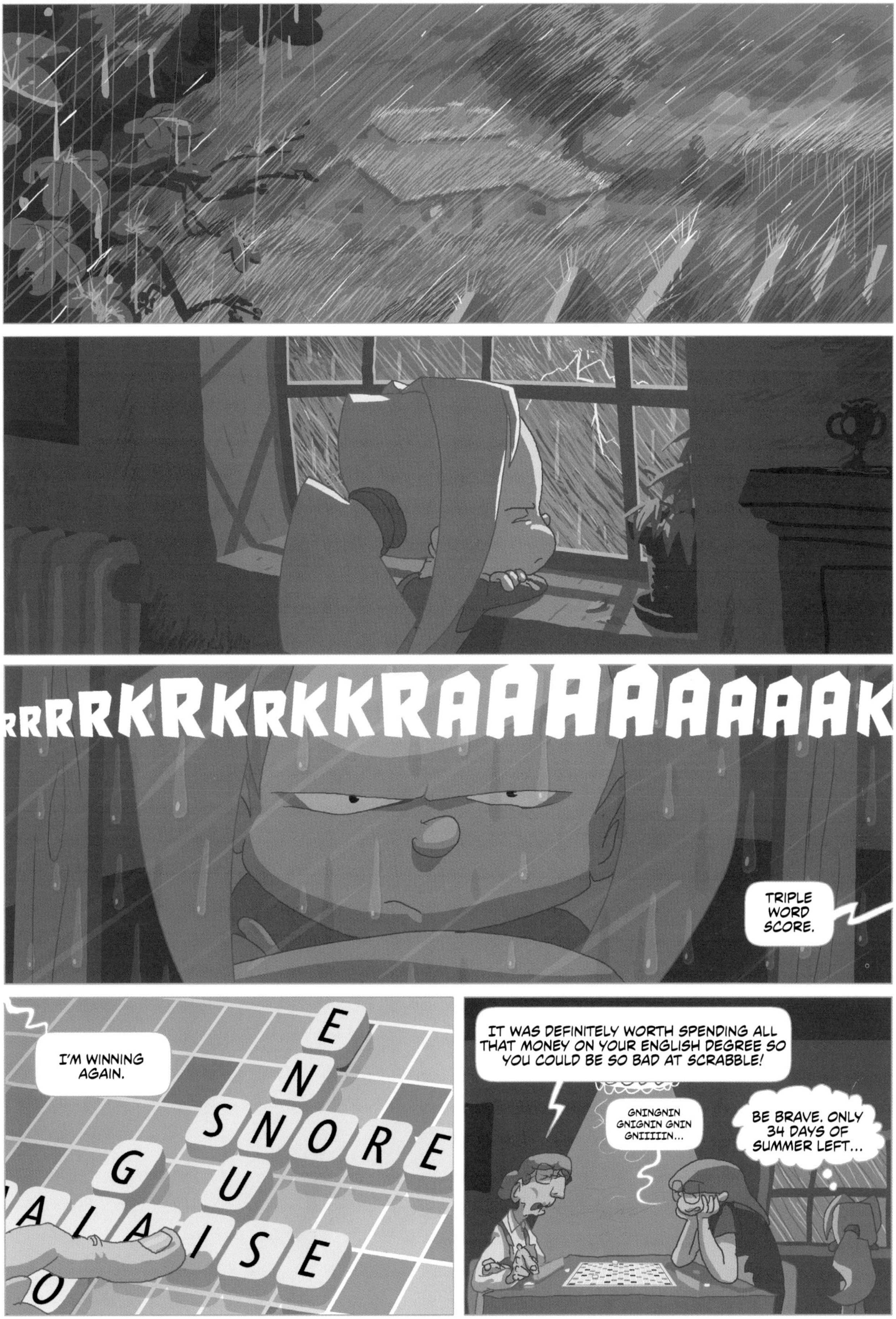
rRRRKRKRKKRAAAAAAAAAK
TRIPLE WORD SCORE.
I'M WINNING AGAIN.
IT WAS DEFINITELY WORTH SPENDING ALL THAT MONEY ON YOUR ENGLISH DEGREE SO YOU COULD BE SO BAD AT SCRABBLE!
GNINGNIN GNIGNIN GNIN GNIIIIIN...
BE BRAVE. ONLY 34 DAYS OF SUMMER LEFT...

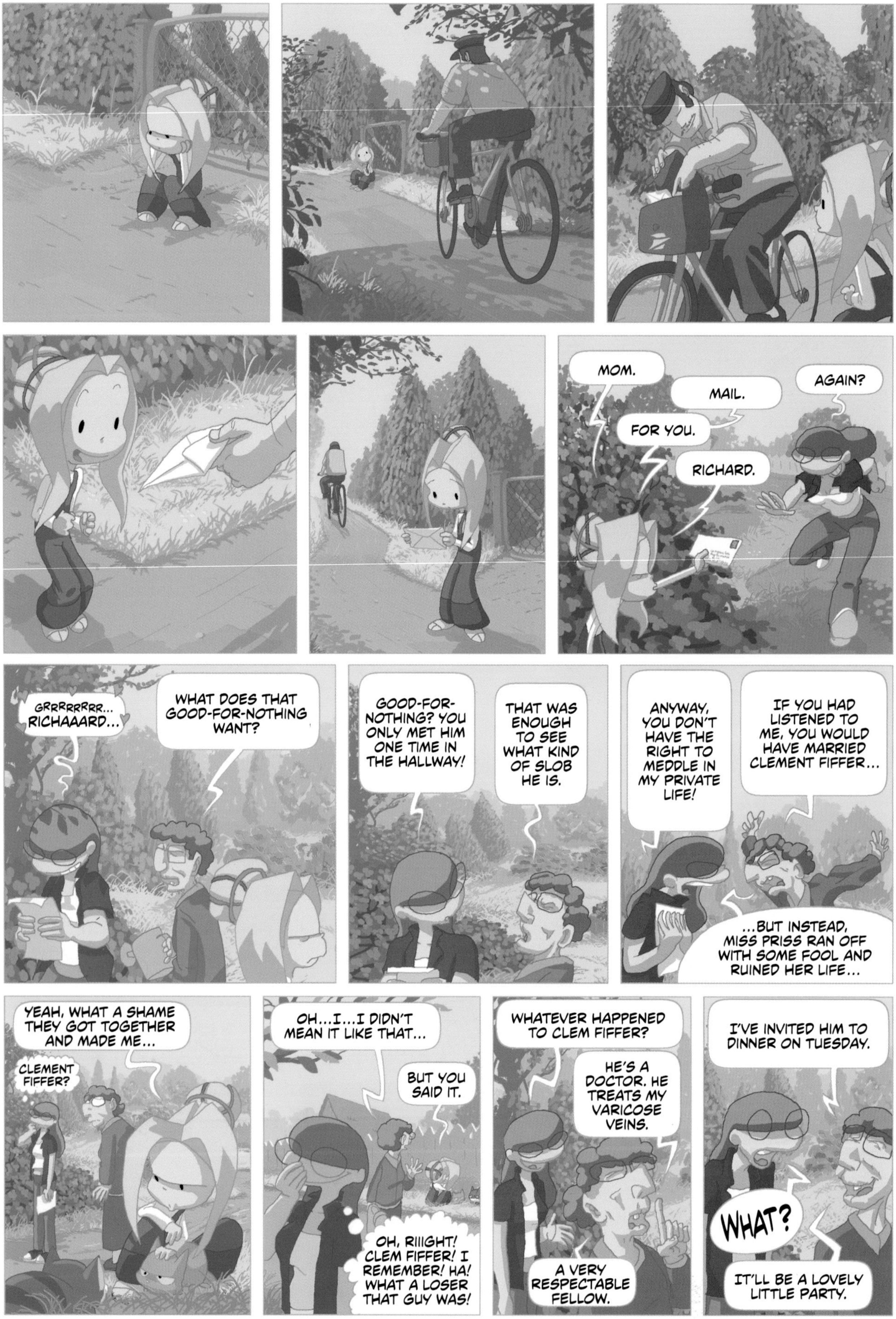
MOM.
MAIL.
FOR YOU.
RICHARD.
AGAIN?
GRRRRRRRR... RICHAAARD...
WHAT DOES THAT GOOD-FOR-NOTHING WANT?
GOOD-FOR-NOTHING? YOU ONLY MET HIM ONE TIME IN THE HALLWAY!
THAT WAS ENOUGH TO SEE WHAT KIND OF SLOB HE IS.
ANYWAY, YOU DON'T HAVE THE RIGHT TO MEDDLE IN MY PRIVATE LIFE!
IF YOU HAD LISTENED TO ME, YOU WOULD HAVE MARRIED CLEMENT FIFFER...
...BUT INSTEAD, MISS PRISS RAN OFF WITH SOME FOOL AND RUINED HER LIFE...
YEAH, WHAT A SHAME THEY GOT TOGETHER AND MADE ME...
CLEMENT FIFFER?
OH...I...I DIDN'T MEAN IT LIKE THAT...
BUT YOU SAID IT.
OH, RIIIGHT! CLEM FIFFER! I REMEMBER! HA! WHAT A LOSER THAT GUY WAS!
WHATEVER HAPPENED TO CLEM FIFFER?
HE'S A DOCTOR. HE TREATS MY VARICOSE VEINS.
A VERY RESPECTABLE FELLOW.
I'VE INVITED HIM TO DINNER ON TUESDAY.
WHAT?
IT'LL BE A LOVELY LITTLE PARTY.

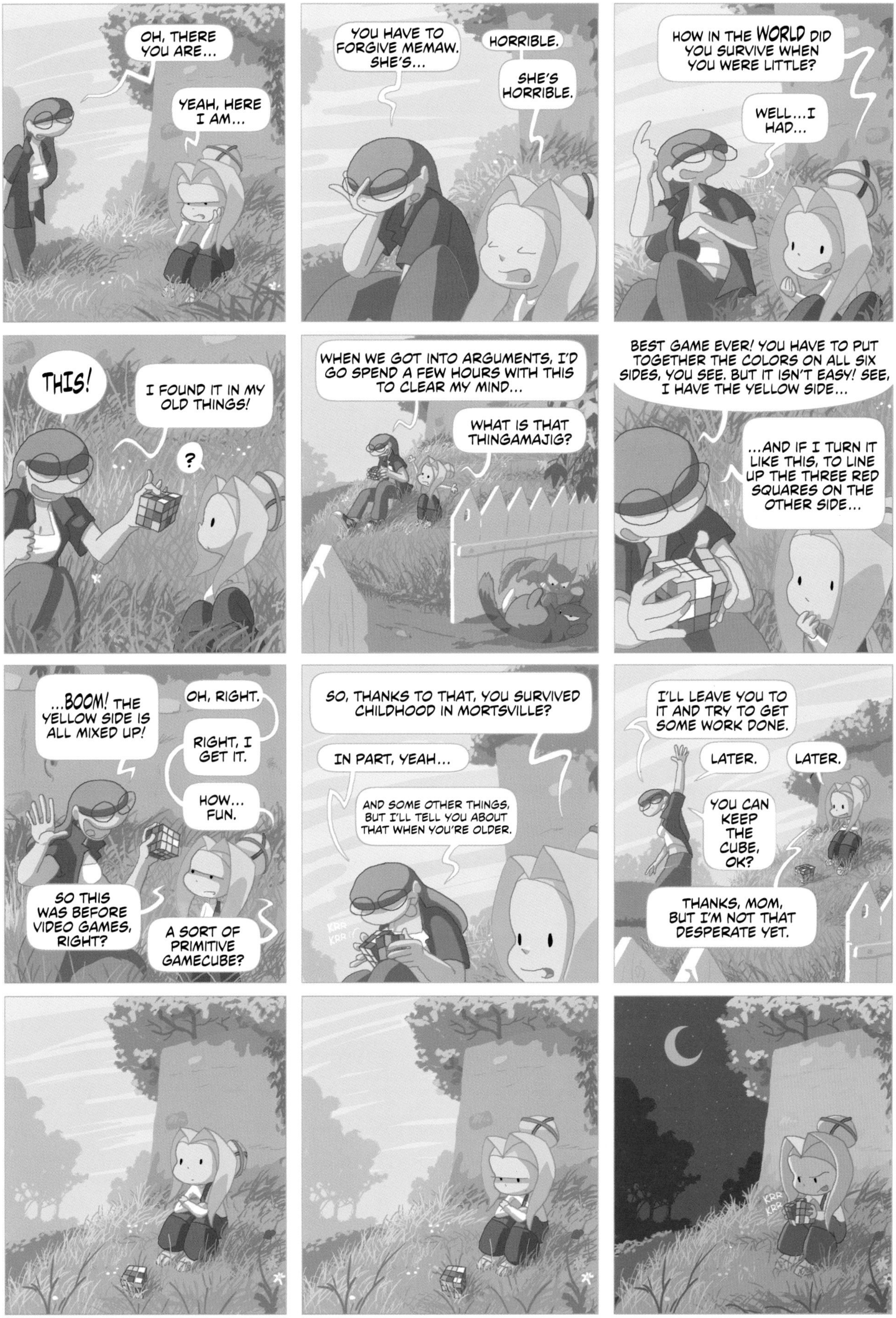
OH, THERE YOU ARE...
YEAH, HERE I AM...
YOU HAVE TO FORGIVE MEMAW. SHE'S...
HORRIBLE.
SHE'S HORRIBLE.
HOW IN THE WORLD DID YOU SURVIVE WHEN YOU WERE LITTLE?
WELL...I HAD...
THIS!
I FOUND IT IN MY OLD THINGS!
?
WHEN WE GOT INTO ARGUMENTS, I'D GO SPEND A FEW HOURS WITH THIS TO CLEAR MY MIND...
WHAT IS THAT THINGAMAJIG?
BEST GAME EVER! YOU HAVE TO PUT TOGETHER THE COLORS ON ALL SIX SIDES, YOU SEE. BUT IT ISN'T EASY! SEE, I HAVE THE YELLOW SIDE...
...AND IF I TURN IT LIKE THIS, TO LINE UP THE THREE RED SQUARES ON THE OTHER SIDE...
...BOOM! THE YELLOW SIDE IS ALL MIXED UP!
OH, RIGHT.
RIGHT, I GET IT.
HOW... FUN.
SO THIS WAS BEFORE VIDEO GAMES, RIGHT?
A SORT OF PRIMITIVE GAMECUBE?
SO, THANKS TO THAT, YOU SURVIVED CHILDHOOD IN MORTSVILLE?
IN PART, YEAH...
AND SOME OTHER THINGS, BUT I'LL TELL YOU ABOUT THAT WHEN YOU'RE OLDER.
KRR KRR
I'LL LEAVE YOU TO IT AND TRY TO GET SOME WORK DONE.
LATER.
LATER.
YOU CAN KEEP THE CUBE, OK?
THANKS, MOM, BUT I'M NOT THAT DESPERATE YET.
KRR KRR

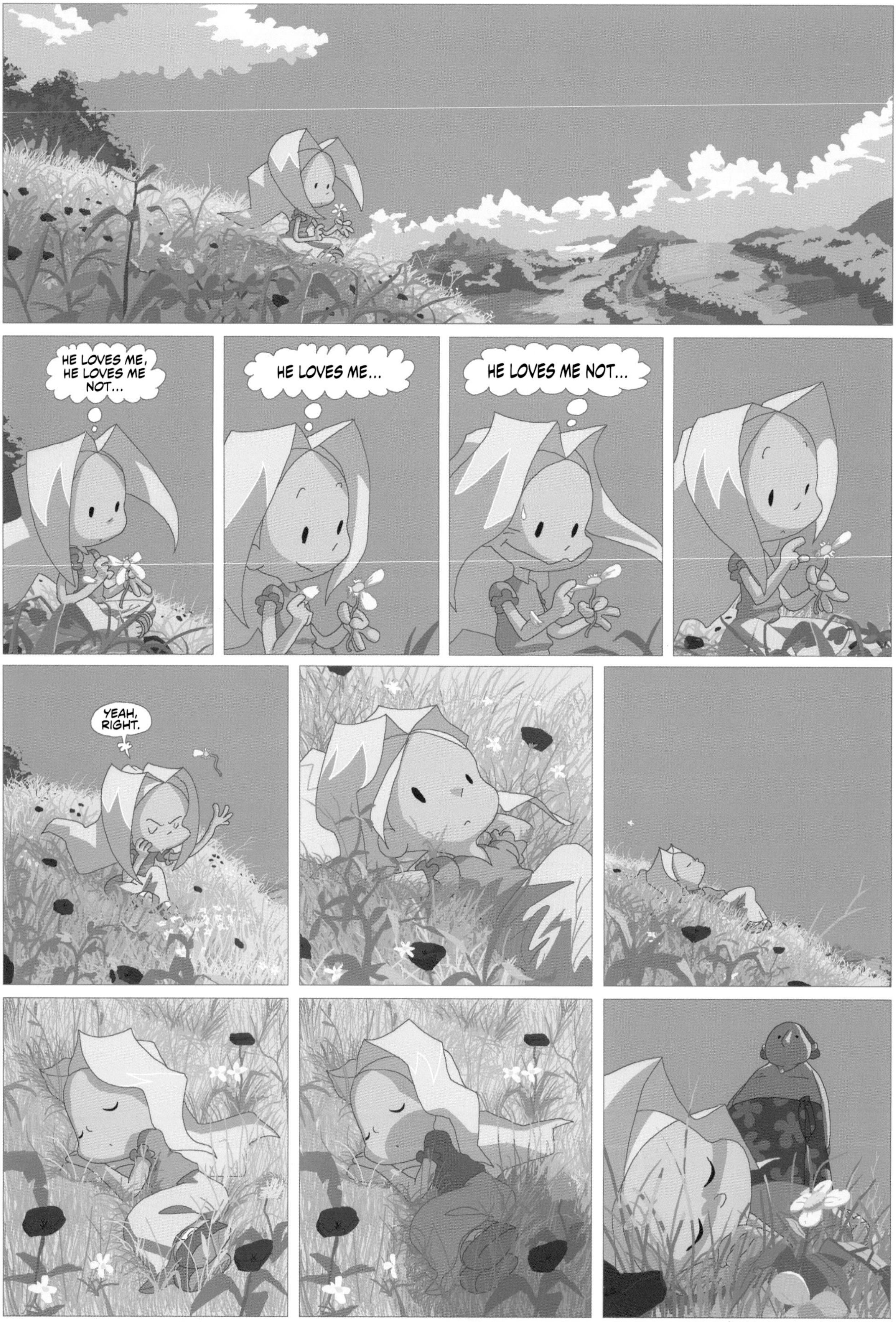
HE LOVES ME, HE LOVES ME NOT...
HE LOVES ME...
HE LOVES ME NOT...
YEAH, RIGHT.

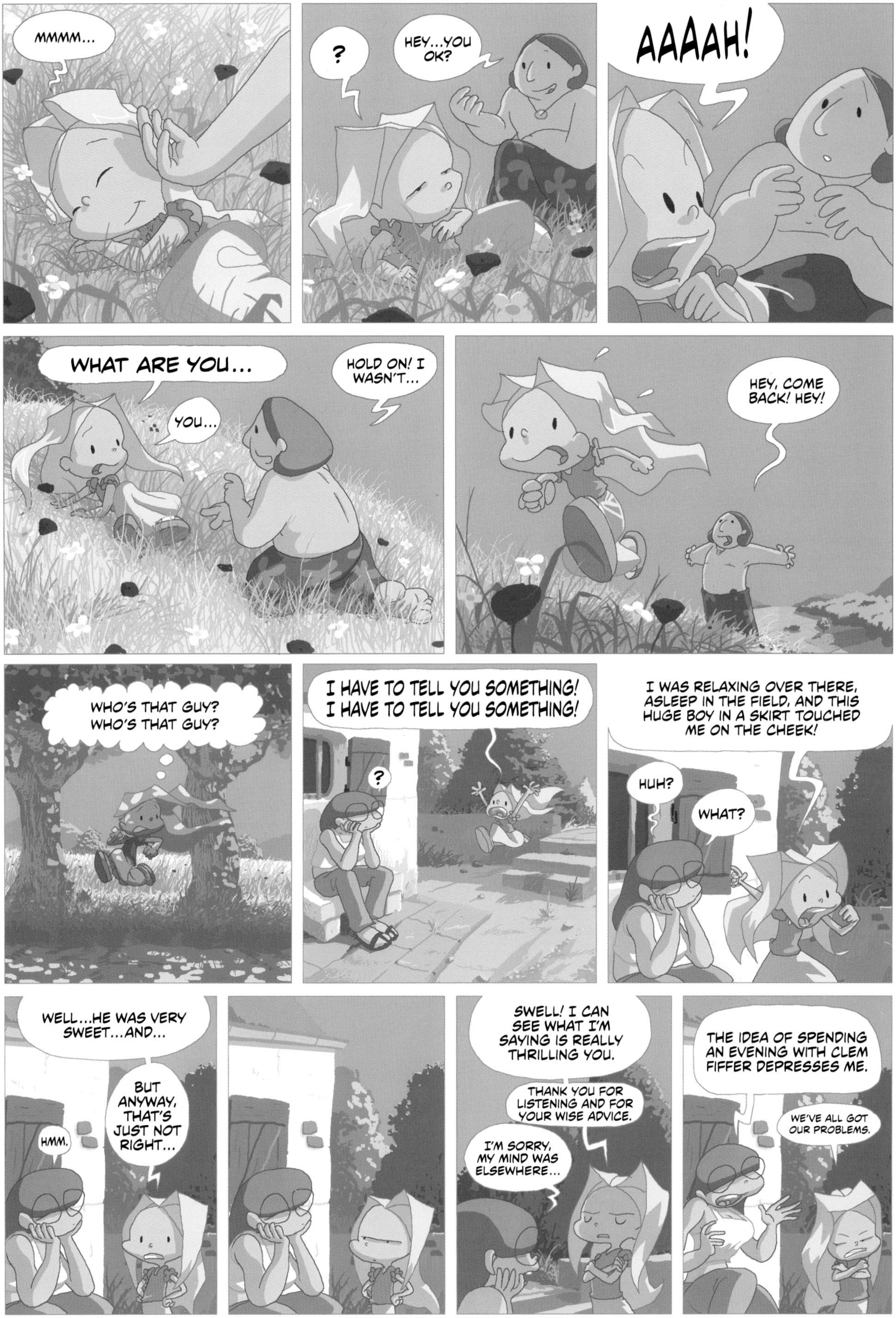
MMMM...
?
HEY...YOU OK?
AAAAH!
WHAT ARE YOU...
YOU...
HOLD ON! I WASN'T...
HEY, COME BACK! HEY!
WHO'S THAT GUY? WHO'S THAT GUY?
I HAVE TO TELL YOU SOMETHING! I HAVE TO TELL YOU SOMETHING!
?
I WAS RELAXING OVER THERE, ASLEEP IN THE FIELD, AND THIS HUGE BOY IN A SKIRT TOUCHED ME ON THE CHEEK!
HUH?
WHAT?
WELL...HE WAS VERY SWEET...AND...
HMM.
BUT ANYWAY, THAT'S JUST NOT RIGHT...
SWELL! I CAN SEE WHAT I'M SAYING IS REALLY THRILLING YOU.
THANK YOU FOR LISTENING AND FOR YOUR WISE ADVICE.
I'M SORRY, MY MIND WAS ELSEWHERE...
THE IDEA OF SPENDING AN EVENING WITH CLEM FIFFER DEPRESSES ME.
WE'VE ALL GOT OUR PROBLEMS.

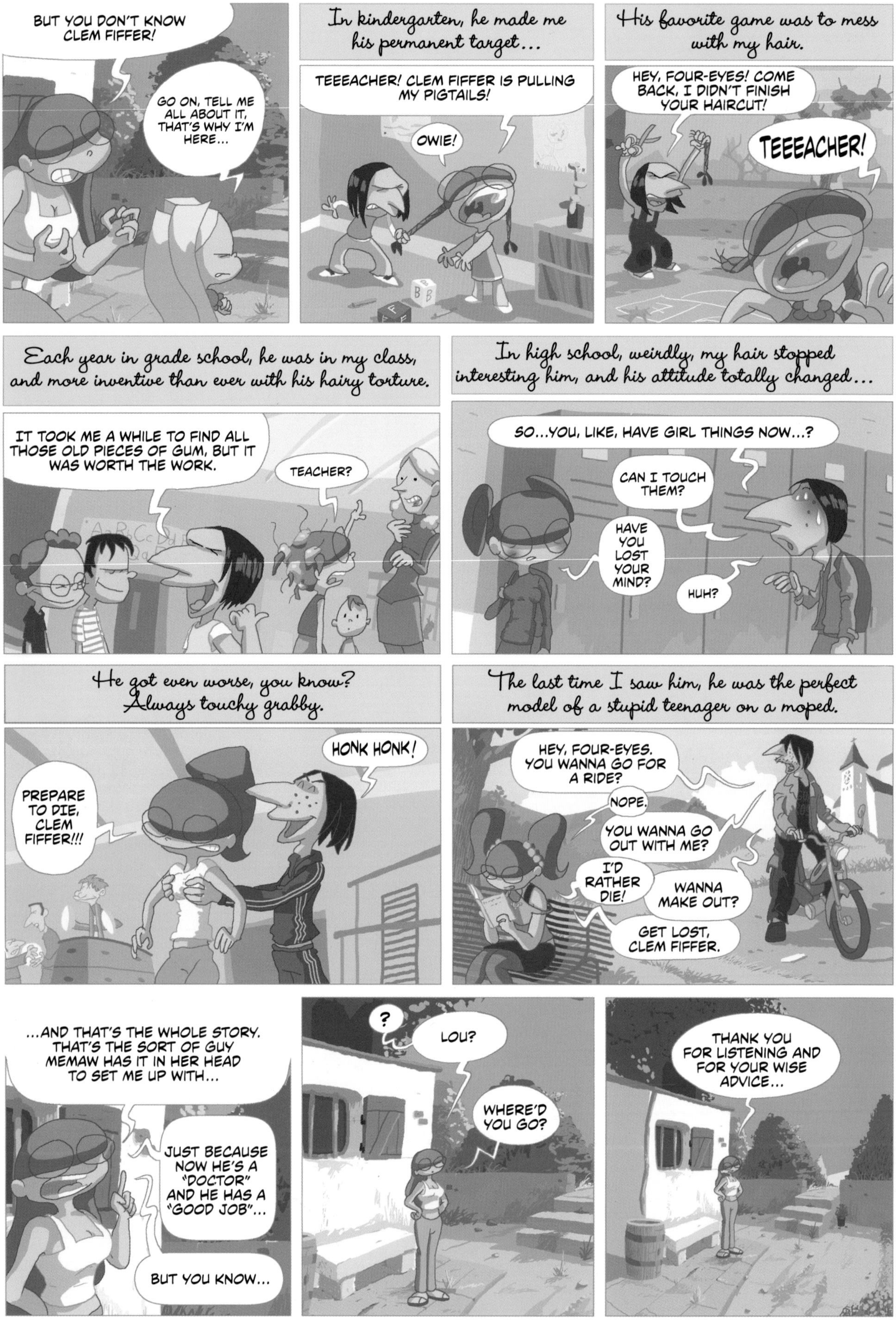

BUT YOU DON'T KNOW CLEM FIFFER!
GO ON, TELL ME ALL ABOUT IT, THAT'S WHY I'M HERE...
In kindergarten, he made me his permanent target...
TEEEACHER! CLEM FIFFER IS PULLING MY PIGTAILS!
OWIE!
His favorite game was to mess with my hair.
HEY, FOUR-EYES! COME BACK, I DIDN'T FINISH YOUR HAIRCUT!
TEEEACHER!
Each year in grade school, he was in my class, and more inventive than ever with his hairy torture.
IT TOOK ME A WHILE TO FIND ALL THOSE OLD PIECES OF GUM, BUT IT WAS WORTH THE WORK.
TEACHER?
In high school, weirdly, my hair stopped interesting him, and his attitude totally changed...
SO...YOU, LIKE, HAVE GIRL THINGS NOW...?
CAN I TOUCH THEM?
HAVE YOU LOST YOUR MIND?
HUH?
He got even worse, you know? Always touchy grabby.
HONK HONK!
PREPARE TO DIE, CLEM FIFFER!!!
The last time I saw him, he was the perfect model of a stupid teenager on a moped.
HEY, FOUR-EYES. YOU WANNA GO FOR A RIDE?
NOPE.
YOU WANNA GO OUT WITH ME?
I'D RATHER DIE!
WANNA MAKE OUT?
GET LOST, CLEM FIFFER.
...AND THAT'S THE WHOLE STORY. THAT'S THE SORT OF GUY MEMAW HAS IT IN HER HEAD TO SET ME UP WITH...
JUST BECAUSE NOW HE'S A "DOCTOR" AND HE HAS A "GOOD JOB"...
BUT YOU KNOW...
?
LOU?
WHERE'D YOU GO?
THANK YOU FOR LISTENING AND FOR YOUR WISE ADVICE...

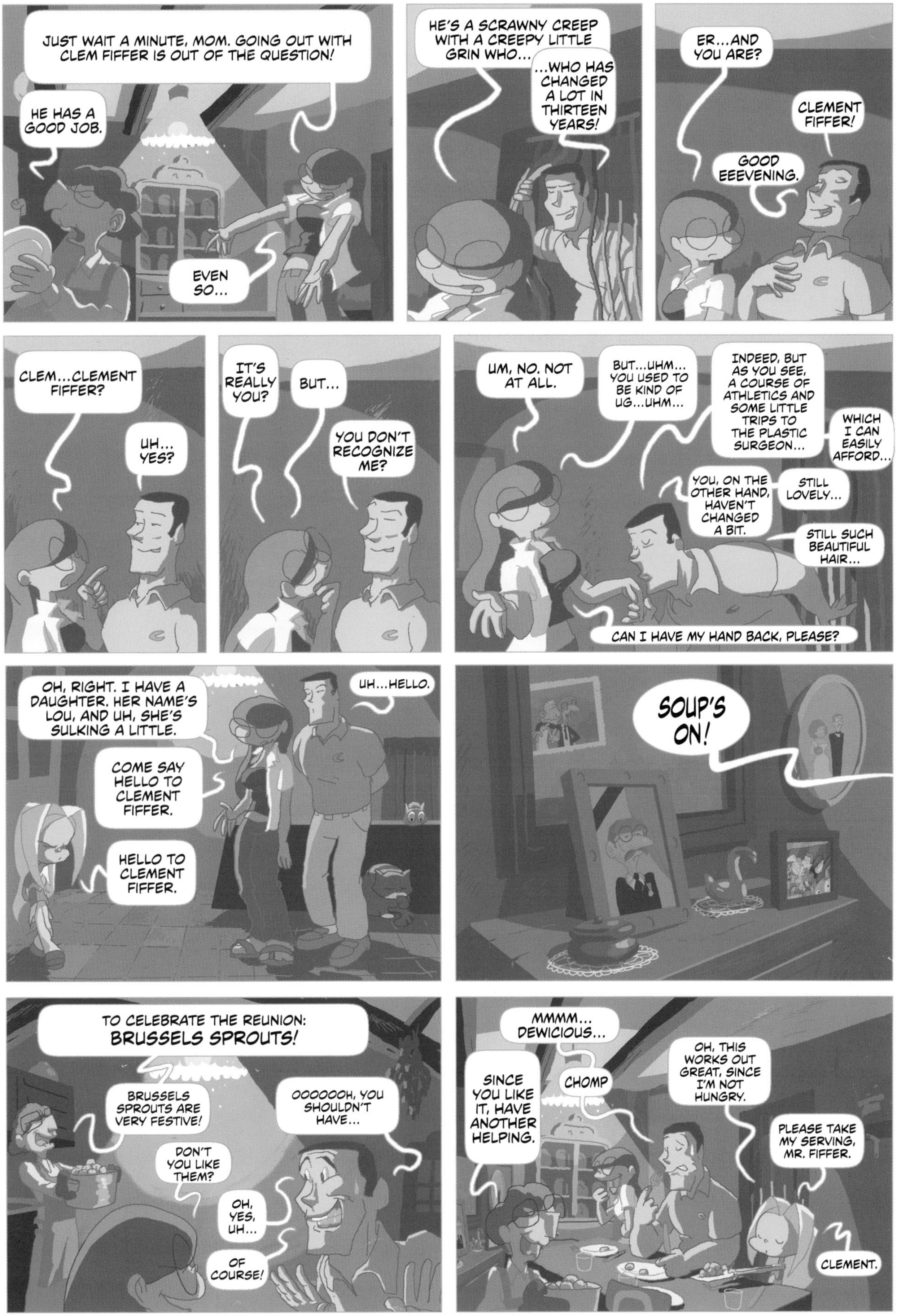
JUST WAIT A MINUTE, MOM. GOING OUT WITH CLEM FIFFER IS OUT OF THE QUESTION!
HE HAS A GOOD JOB.
EVEN SO...
HE'S A SCRAWNY CREEP WITH A CREEPY LITTLE GRIN WHO...
...WHO HAS CHANGED A LOT IN THIRTEEN YEARS!
ER...AND YOU ARE?
CLEMENT FIFFER!
GOOD EEEVENING.
CLEM...CLEMENT FIFFER?
UH... YES?
IT'S REALLY YOU?
BUT...
YOU DON'T RECOGNIZE ME?
UM, NO. NOT AT ALL.
BUT...UHM... YOU USED TO BE KIND OF UG...UHM...
INDEED, BUT AS YOU SEE, A COURSE OF ATHLETICS AND SOME LITTLE TRIPS TO THE PLASTIC SURGEON...
WHICH I CAN EASILY AFFORD...
YOU, ON THE OTHER HAND, HAVEN'T CHANGED A BIT.
STILL LOVELY...
STILL SUCH BEAUTIFUL HAIR...
CAN I HAVE MY HAND BACK, PLEASE?
OH, RIGHT. I HAVE A DAUGHTER. HER NAME'S LOU, AND UH, SHE'S SULKING A LITTLE.
UH...HELLO.
COME SAY HELLO TO CLEMENT FIFFER.
HELLO TO CLEMENT FIFFER.
SOUP'S ON!
TO CELEBRATE THE REUNION: BRUSSELS SPROUTS!
BRUSSELS SPROUTS ARE VERY FESTIVE!
OOOOOOH, YOU SHOULDN'T HAVE...
DON'T YOU LIKE THEM?
OH, YES, UH...
OF COURSE!
MMMM... DEWICIOUS...
CHOMP
SINCE YOU LIKE IT, HAVE ANOTHER HELPING.
OH, THIS WORKS OUT GREAT, SINCE I'M NOT HUNGRY.
PLEASE TAKE MY SERVING, MR. FIFFER.
CLEMENT.

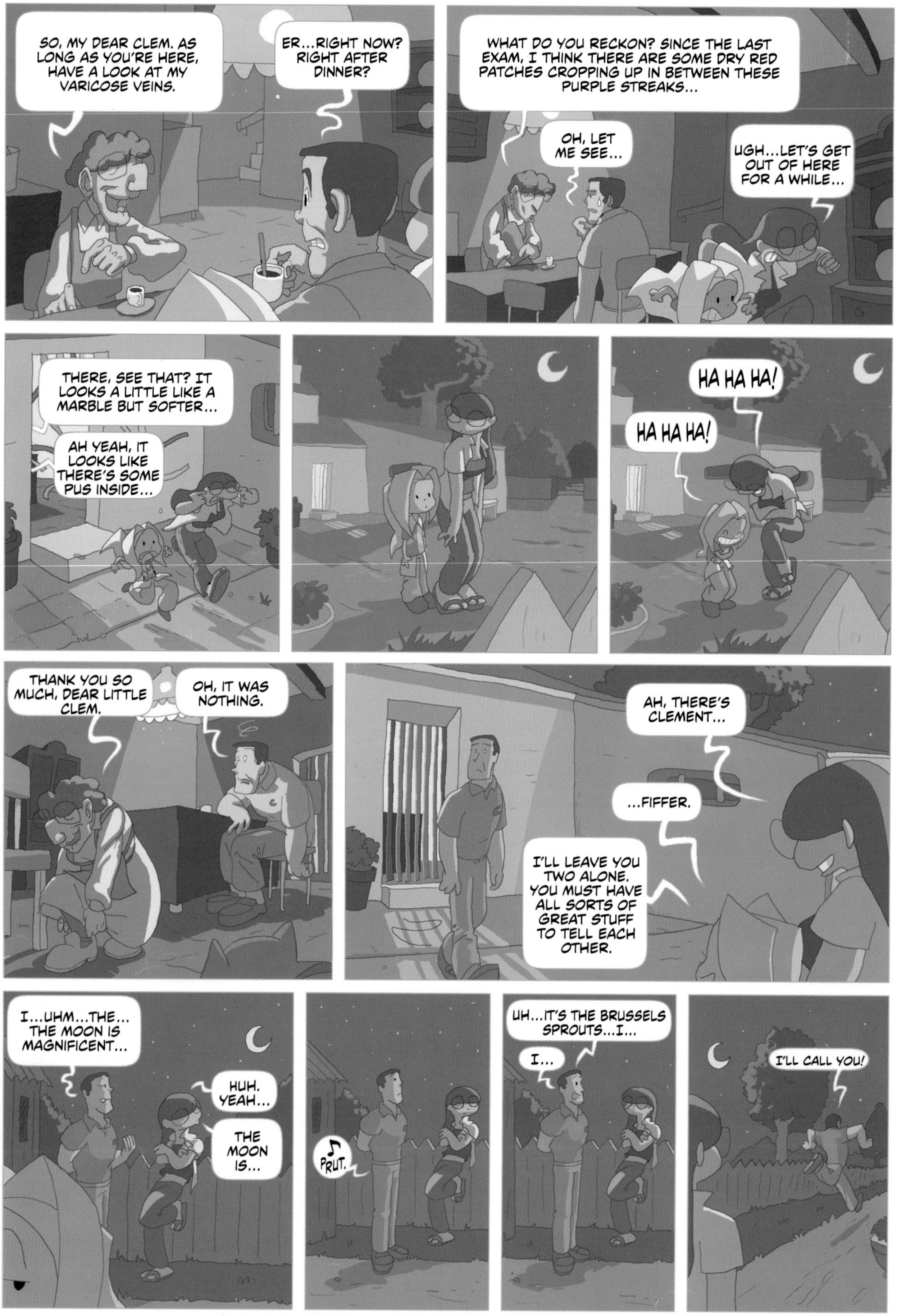

SO, MY DEAR CLEM. AS LONG AS YOU'RE HERE, HAVE A LOOK AT MY VARICOSE VEINS.
ER...RIGHT NOW? RIGHT AFTER DINNER?
WHAT DO YOU RECKON? SINCE THE LAST EXAM, I THINK THERE ARE SOME DRY RED PATCHES CROPPING UP IN BETWEEN THESE PURPLE STREAKS...
OH, LET ME SEE...
UGH...LET'S GET OUT OF HERE FOR A WHILE...
THERE, SEE THAT? IT LOOKS A LITTLE LIKE A MARBLE BUT SOFTER...
AH YEAH, IT LOOKS LIKE THERE'S SOME PUS INSIDE...
HA HA HA!
HA HA HA!
THANK YOU SO MUCH, DEAR LITTLE CLEM.
OH, IT WAS NOTHING.
AH, THERE'S CLEMENT...
...FIFFER.
I'LL LEAVE YOU TWO ALONE. YOU MUST HAVE ALL SORTS OF GREAT STUFF TO TELL EACH OTHER.
I...UHM...THE... THE MOON IS MAGNIFICENT...
HUH. YEAH...
THE MOON IS...
PRUT.
UH...IT'S THE BRUSSELS SPROUTS...I...
I...
I'LL CALL YOU!

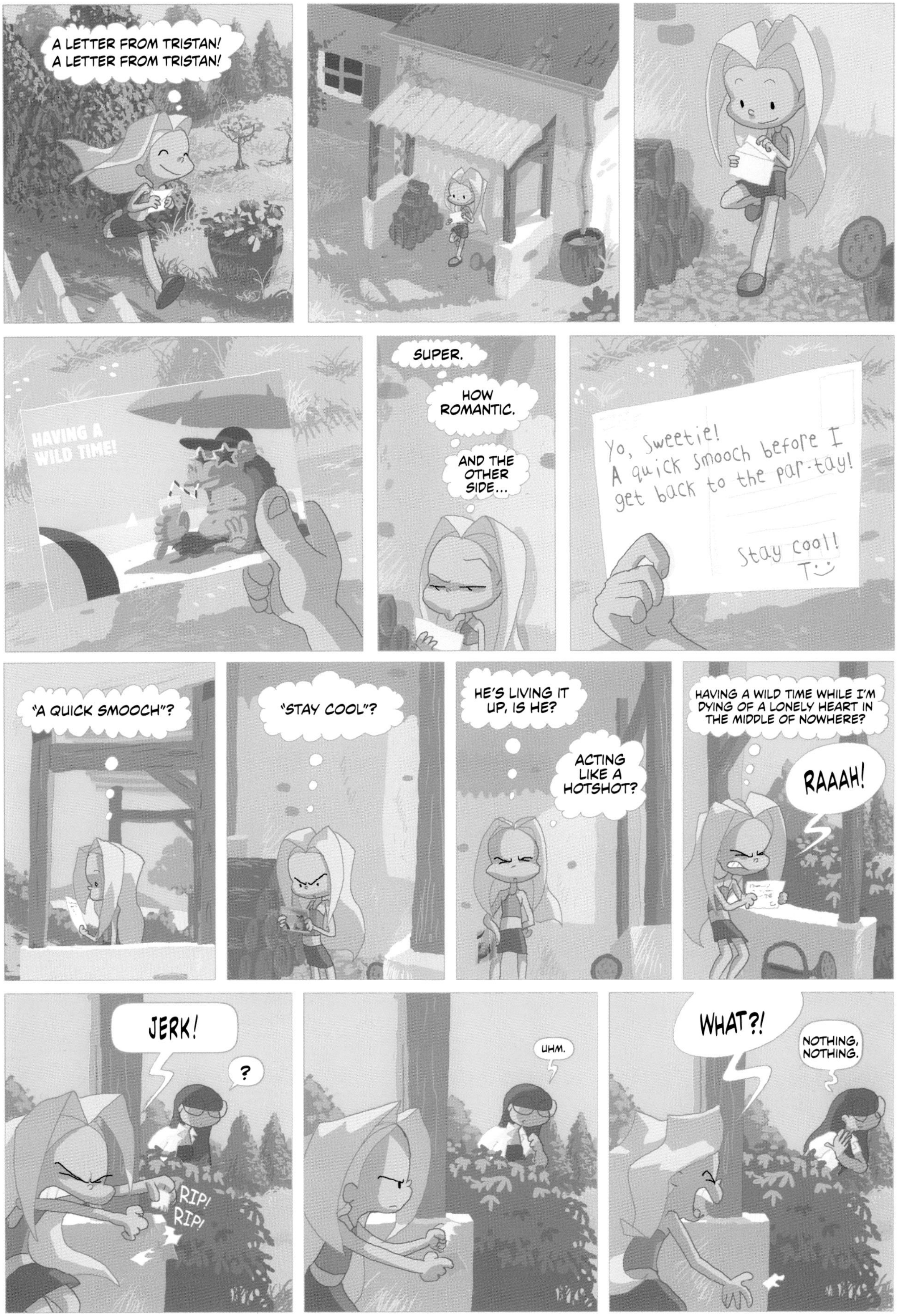
A LETTER FROM TRISTAN!
A LETTER FROM TRISTAN!
HAVING A WILD TIME!
SUPER.
HOW ROMANTIC.
AND THE OTHER SIDE...
Yo, Sweetie!
A quick smooch before I get back to the par-tay!
Stay cool!
T
"A QUICK SMOOCH"?
"STAY COOL"?
HE'S LIVING IT UP, IS HE?
ACTING LIKE A HOTSHOT?
HAVING A WILD TIME WHILE I'M DYING OF A LONELY HEART IN THE MIDDLE OF NOWHERE?
RAAAH!
JERK!
?
RIP!
RIP!
UHM.
WHAT?!
NOTHING, NOTHING.

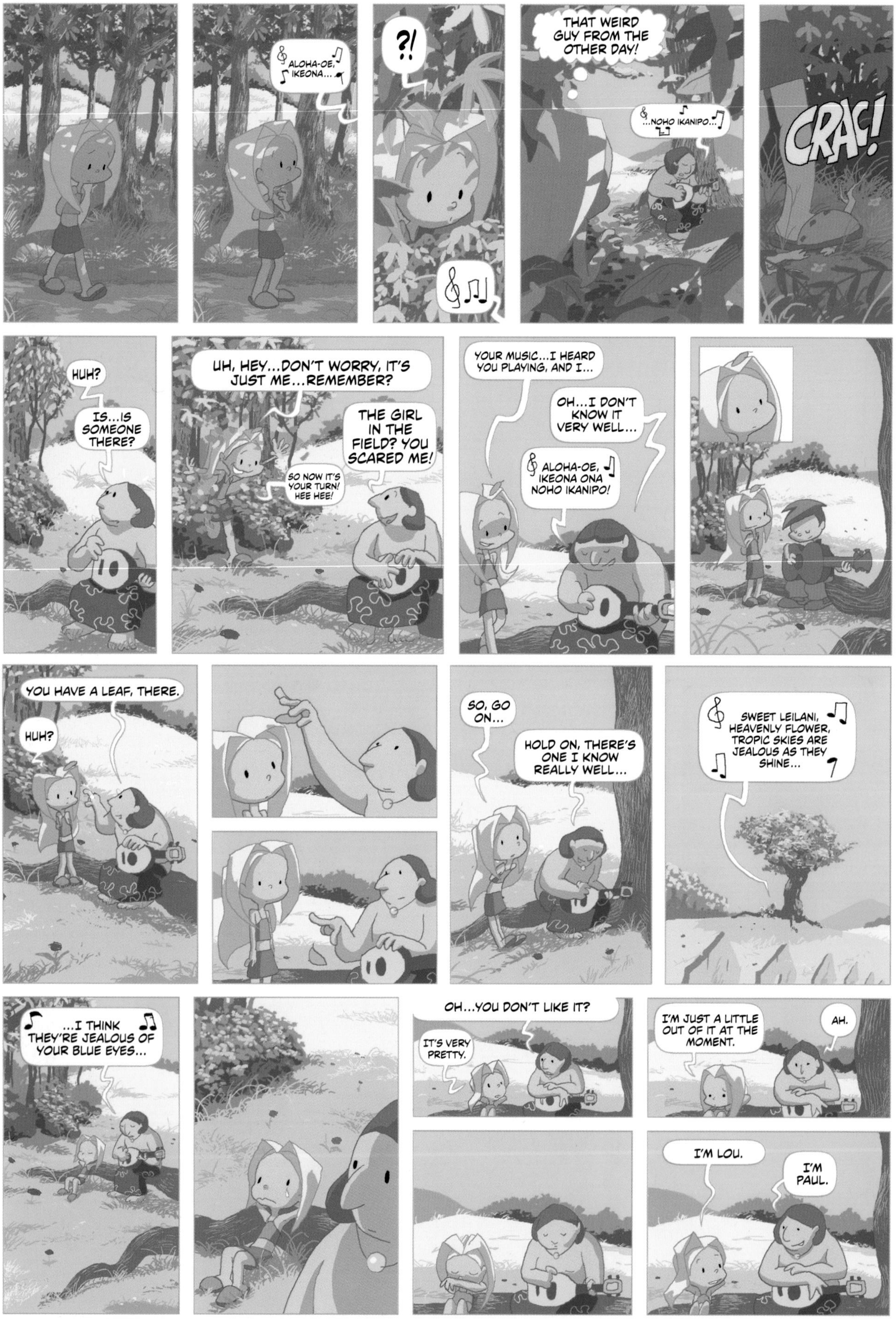
ALOHA-OE, IKEONA...
?!
THAT WEIRD GUY FROM THE OTHER DAY!
...NOHO IKANIPO...
CRAC!
HUH?
IS...IS SOMEONE THERE?
UH, HEY...DON'T WORRY, IT'S JUST ME...REMEMBER?
SO NOW IT'S YOUR TURN! HEE HEE!
THE GIRL IN THE FIELD? YOU SCARED ME!
YOUR MUSIC...I HEARD YOU PLAYING, AND I...
OH...I DON'T KNOW IT VERY WELL...
ALOHA-OE, IKEONA ONA NOHO IKANIPO!
YOU HAVE A LEAF, THERE.
HUH?
SO, GO ON...
HOLD ON, THERE'S ONE I KNOW REALLY WELL...
SWEET LEILANI, HEAVENLY FLOWER, TROPIC SKIES ARE JEALOUS AS THEY SHINE...
...I THINK THEY'RE JEALOUS OF YOUR BLUE EYES...
OH...YOU DON'T LIKE IT?
IT'S VERY PRETTY.
I'M JUST A LITTLE OUT OF IT AT THE MOMENT.
AH.
I'M LOU.
I'M PAUL.

OH, LOOK, IT'S TIME FOR MY SOAP...

BLASTED CONTRAPTION!

OOF, MY BACK.

KRAAKT

KSLIPIKSLIPIKSLIP!

AND OF COURSE I DON'T HAVE MY GOOD READING GLASSES...

WHAT'S WRONG WITH THIS IRRITATING MACHINE.

LET'S SEE HERE...

THEY FILL OUR DREAMS! THEY TURN OUR HEADS!

LOOOVE FAAAAME BEEAAUUUTYYY
DUMDEDUMDEDUMDEDUM

THEY FILL OUR DREAMS! THEY TURN OUR HEADS!

YEAH, THAT'S IT!

LOOOVE FAAAAME BEEAAUUUTYYY!
DUMDEDUMDEDUMDEDUM
THEY SET US FREE!

KSLIPIKSLIPIKSLIP!

INHERIT IT OR WIN IT! BEG, BORROW, STEAL IT!

USELESS THINGAMAJIG...

So you see, Ridge, I knew that Brooke was trying to ruin me by bragging publicly about Eric Forrester's tricks...

HMPH. THAT BROOKE IS SUCH A COW.

But I wasn't fooled. I knew that Stephanie suspected that it was Duncan who was pulling the strings so he could have Sheila committed...

HMFR...

He hoped that Sally wouldn't recover her memory. She could prove that Jamie gave false evidence in court that Rickie is the evil twin of Clarkie, the notary public and the mistress hid the money...

ZZZZZZZZZZZZ.

LOOOVE FAAAAME BEEAAUUUTYYY
DUM

ZZZ? HM WUH? HUH?! WHAT?!

THEY FILL OUR DREAMS! THEY TURN OUR HEADS!

OH, GOOD, IT'S FINALLY OVER.

OOF, MY BACK.

KRAAK

LOOOVE FAAAAME BEEAAUUUTYYY!
DUMDEDUMDEDUMDEDUM
THEY SET US FREE!

ASININE.

KSLIPIKSLIPIKSLIP!

INHERIT IT OR.....

TIC

BLASTED CONTRAPTION.

KSLIPIKSLIP!

WHAT A GREAT INVENTION!

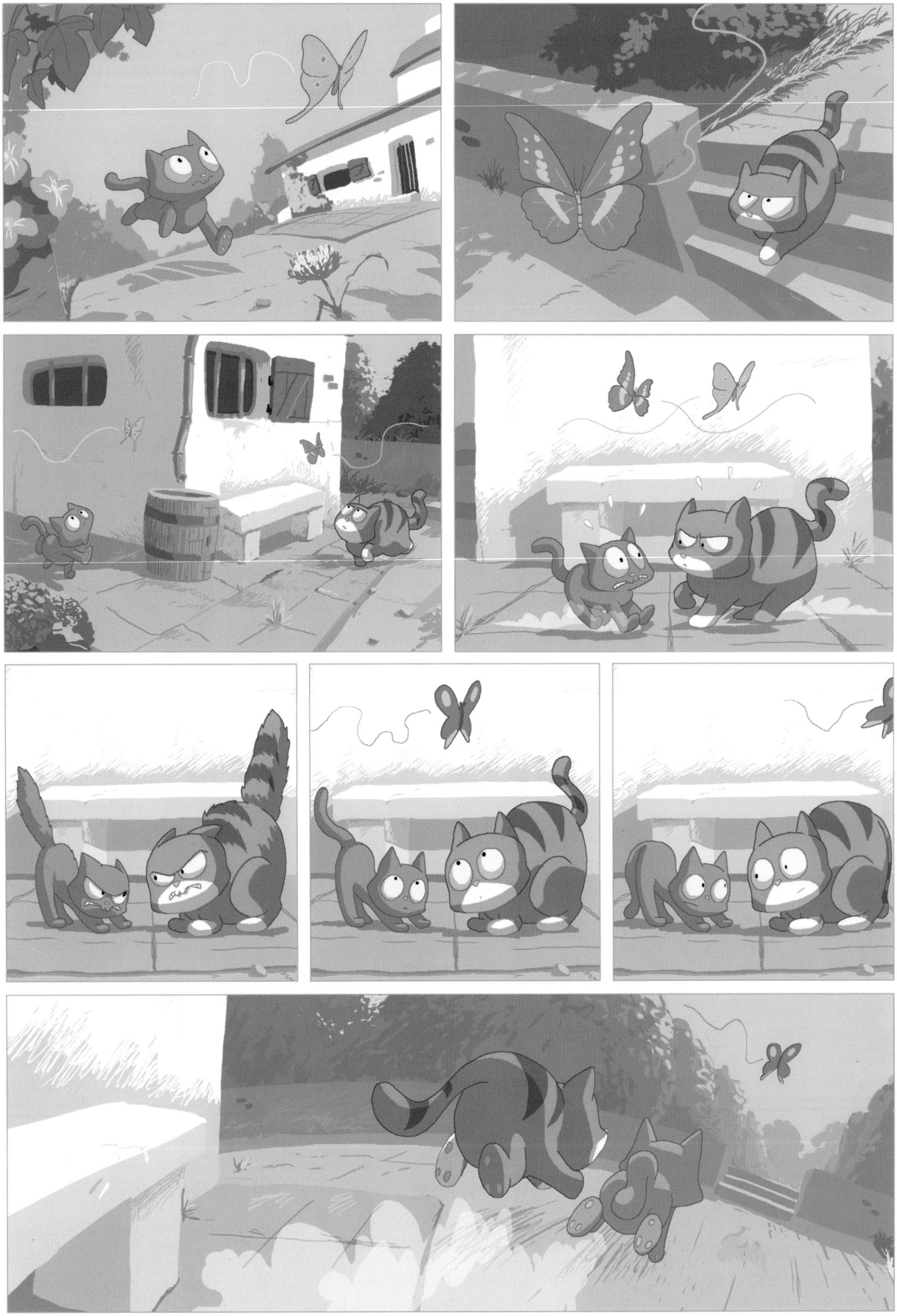

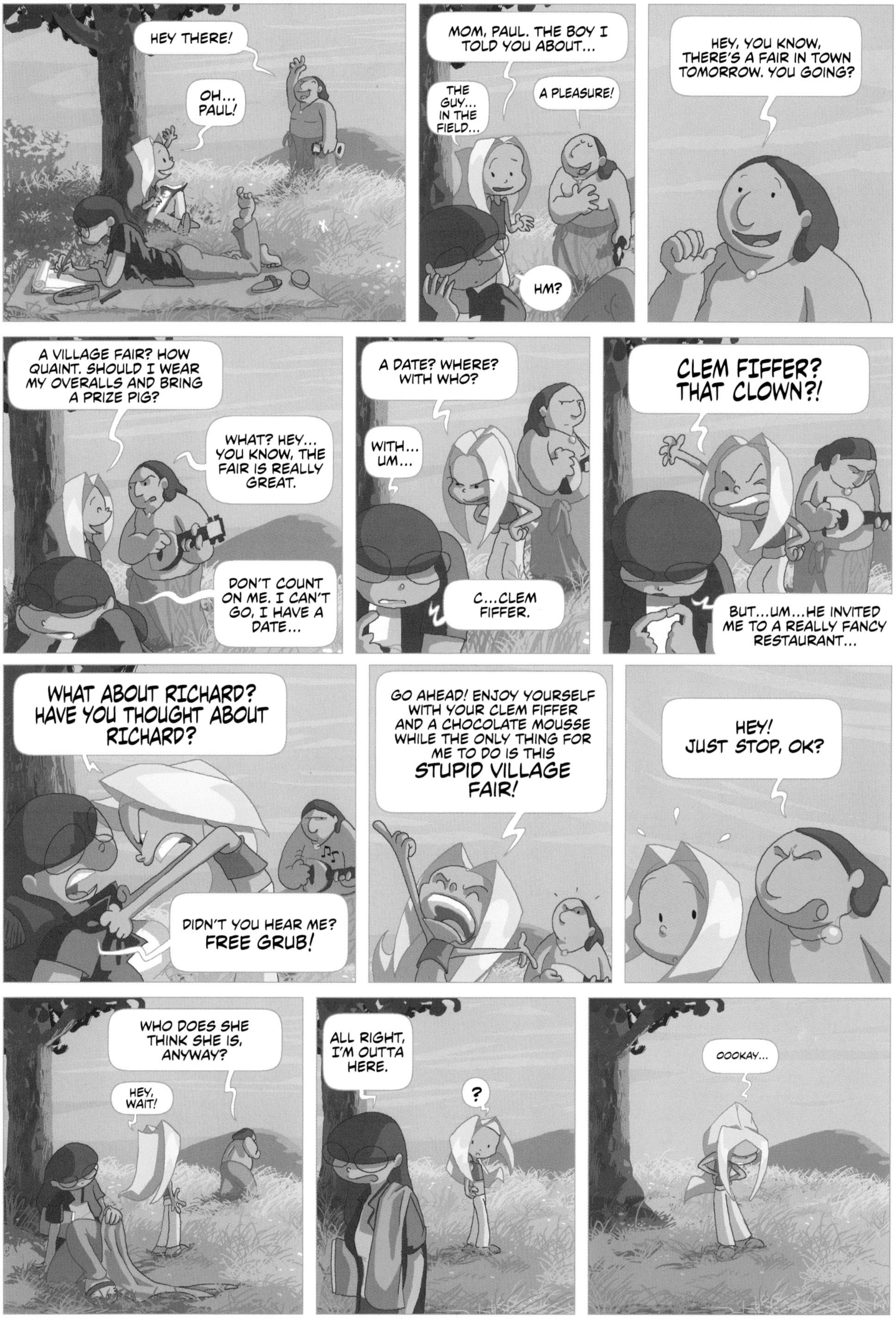
HEY THERE!
OH... PAUL!
MOM, PAUL. THE BOY I TOLD YOU ABOUT...
THE GUY... IN THE FIELD...
A PLEASURE!
HM?
HEY, YOU KNOW, THERE'S A FAIR IN TOWN TOMORROW. YOU GOING?
A VILLAGE FAIR? HOW QUAINT. SHOULD I WEAR MY OVERALLS AND BRING A PRIZE PIG?
WHAT? HEY... YOU KNOW, THE FAIR IS REALLY GREAT.
DON'T COUNT ON ME. I CAN'T GO, I HAVE A DATE...
A DATE? WHERE? WITH WHO?
WITH... UM...
C...CLEM FIFFER.
CLEM FIFFER? THAT CLOWN?!
BUT...UM...HE INVITED ME TO A REALLY FANCY RESTAURANT...
WHAT ABOUT RICHARD? HAVE YOU THOUGHT ABOUT RICHARD?
DIDN'T YOU HEAR ME? FREE GRUB!
GO AHEAD! ENJOY YOURSELF WITH YOUR CLEM FIFFER AND A CHOCOLATE MOUSSE WHILE THE ONLY THING FOR ME TO DO IS THIS STUPID VILLAGE FAIR!
HEY! JUST STOP, OK?
WHO DOES SHE THINK SHE IS, ANYWAY?
HEY, WAIT!
ALL RIGHT, I'M OUTTA HERE.
?
OOOKAY...

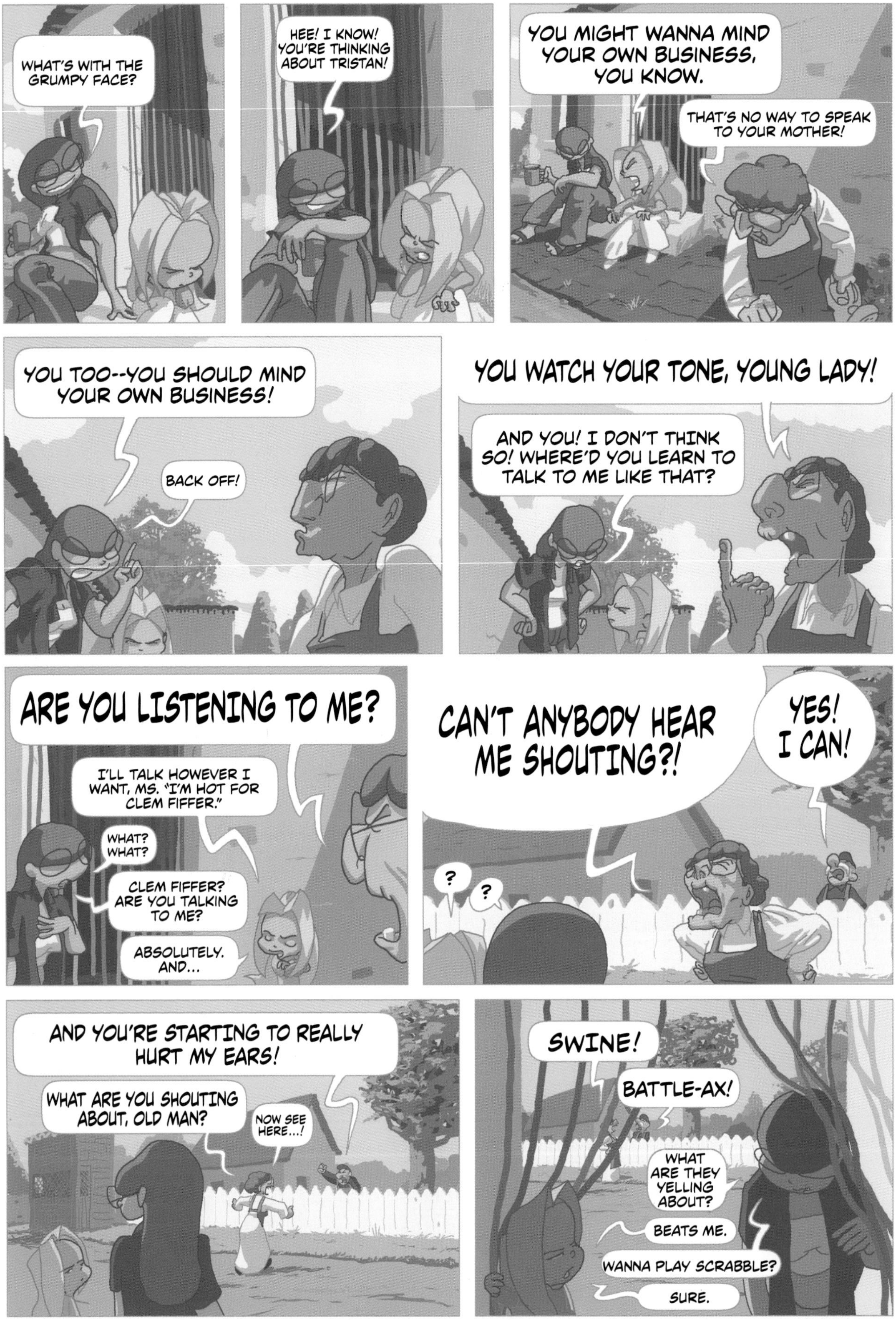
WHAT'S WITH THE GRUMPY FACE?
HEE! I KNOW! YOU'RE THINKING ABOUT TRISTAN!
YOU MIGHT WANNA MIND YOUR OWN BUSINESS, YOU KNOW.
THAT'S NO WAY TO SPEAK TO YOUR MOTHER!
YOU TOO--YOU SHOULD MIND YOUR OWN BUSINESS!
BACK OFF!
YOU WATCH YOUR TONE, YOUNG LADY!
AND YOU! I DON'T THINK SO! WHERE'D YOU LEARN TO TALK TO ME LIKE THAT?
ARE YOU LISTENING TO ME?
I'LL TALK HOWEVER I WANT, MS. "I'M HOT FOR CLEM FIFFER."
WHAT? WHAT?
CLEM FIFFER? ARE YOU TALKING TO ME?
ABSOLUTELY. AND...
CAN'T ANYBODY HEAR ME SHOUTING?!
YES! I CAN!
?
?
AND YOU'RE STARTING TO REALLY HURT MY EARS!
WHAT ARE YOU SHOUTING ABOUT, OLD MAN?
NOW SEE HERE...!
SWINE!
BATTLE-AX!
WHAT ARE THEY YELLING ABOUT?
BEATS ME.
WANNA PLAY SCRABBLE?
SURE.

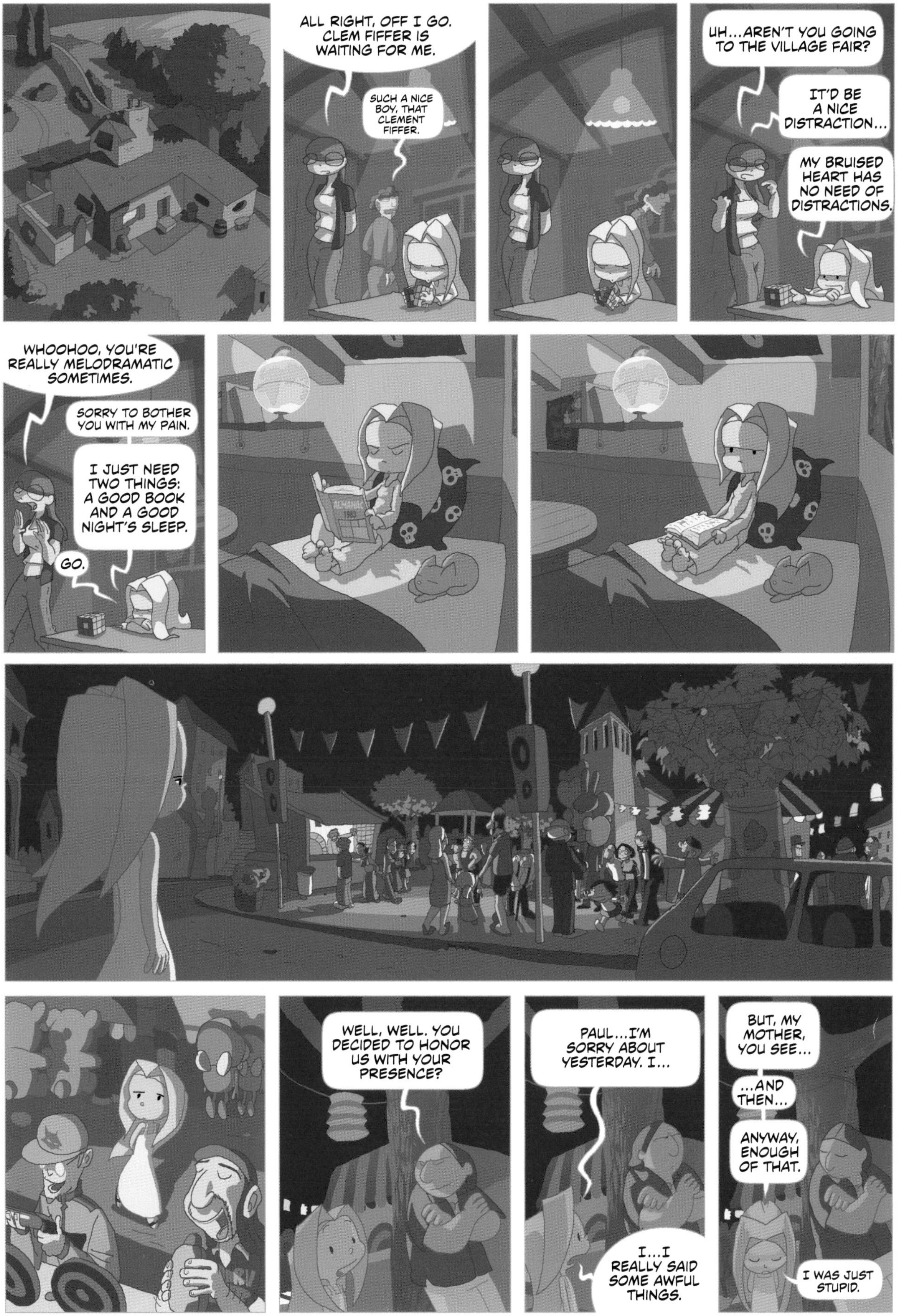
ALL RIGHT, OFF I GO. CLEM FIFFER IS WAITING FOR ME.
SUCH A NICE BOY, THAT CLEMENT FIFFER.
UH...AREN'T YOU GOING TO THE VILLAGE FAIR?
IT'D BE A NICE DISTRACTION...
MY BRUISED HEART HAS NO NEED OF DISTRACTIONS.
WHOOHOO, YOU'RE REALLY MELODRAMATIC SOMETIMES.
SORRY TO BOTHER YOU WITH MY PAIN.
I JUST NEED TWO THINGS: A GOOD BOOK AND A GOOD NIGHT'S SLEEP.
GO.
ALMANAC 1983
WELL, WELL. YOU DECIDED TO HONOR US WITH YOUR PRESENCE?
PAUL...I'M SORRY ABOUT YESTERDAY. I...
I...I REALLY SAID SOME AWFUL THINGS.
BUT, MY MOTHER, YOU SEE...
...AND THEN...
ANYWAY, ENOUGH OF THAT.
I WAS JUST STUPID.

LOOK...FOLLOW ME. I KNOW SOMETHING THAT'LL CHEER YOU UP.

?

ATTENTION! EVERYONE TAKE YOUR PLACES FOR THE TANGO WITH AMADEUS AND HIS MAGIC ACCORDION!

MY LADY, WOULD YOU SHARE A DANCE WITH A POOR COMMONER?

HEE HEE!

DON'T WORRY. I THINK THE FAIR IS A LITTLE OLD-FASHIONED TOO.

PFFT...

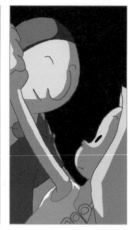

LOBSTER BISQUE WITH FRESH FOIE GRAS IN A VINTAGE COGNAC SAUCE.

♪ OOOOOOH ♫

OH.

ENJOY! I SUPPOSE WITH YOUR LITTLE BOOKS YOU DON'T EARN ENOUGH FOR THIS KIND OF RESTAURANT!

OR SUCH FINE WINES.

HA HA!

YEAH, AND YOU. YOU SURE ARE CLASSY.

...AND THEN MADAGASCAR! OOH LA LA! MAGNIFICENT! BUT YOU CAN'T IMAGINE THE SQUALOR THE PEOPLE THERE LIVE IN...

IT'S VERY EXOTIC!

YOU KNOW, I MAY BE SUCCESSFUL BUT I LIKE TO KEEP MY LIFE SIMPLE. FOR EXAMPLE: WHEN I BOUGHT MY HUMVEE, I DIDN'T GET THE CHROME RIMS.

OH, YES, WHAT A BIG HEART YOU HAVE.

ANY WINE LEFT?

GARÇON! WITH OUR DESSERT: CHAMPAGNE!

YES, SOMETHING TO WASH IT DOWN, WOULDN'T WANT YOU TO CHOKE ON IT.

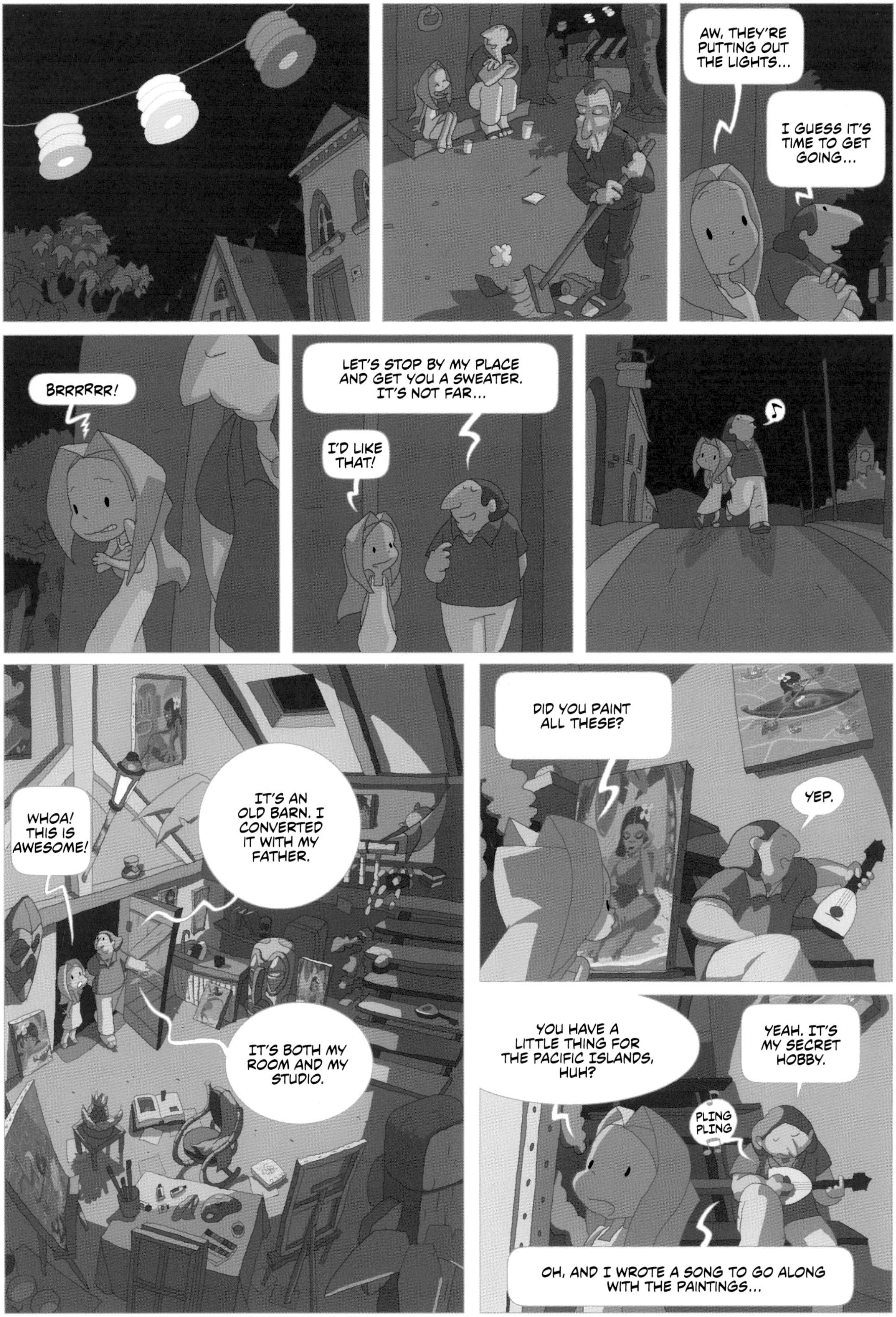
AW, THEY'RE PUTTING OUT THE LIGHTS...
I GUESS IT'S TIME TO GET GOING...
BRRRRRR!
LET'S STOP BY MY PLACE AND GET YOU A SWEATER. IT'S NOT FAR...
I'D LIKE THAT!
♪
WHOA! THIS IS AWESOME!
IT'S AN OLD BARN. I CONVERTED IT WITH MY FATHER.
IT'S BOTH MY ROOM AND MY STUDIO.
DID YOU PAINT ALL THESE?
YEP.
YOU HAVE A LITTLE THING FOR THE PACIFIC ISLANDS, HUH?
YEAH. IT'S MY SECRET HOBBY.
PLING PLING
OH, AND I WROTE A SONG TO GO ALONG WITH THE PAINTINGS...

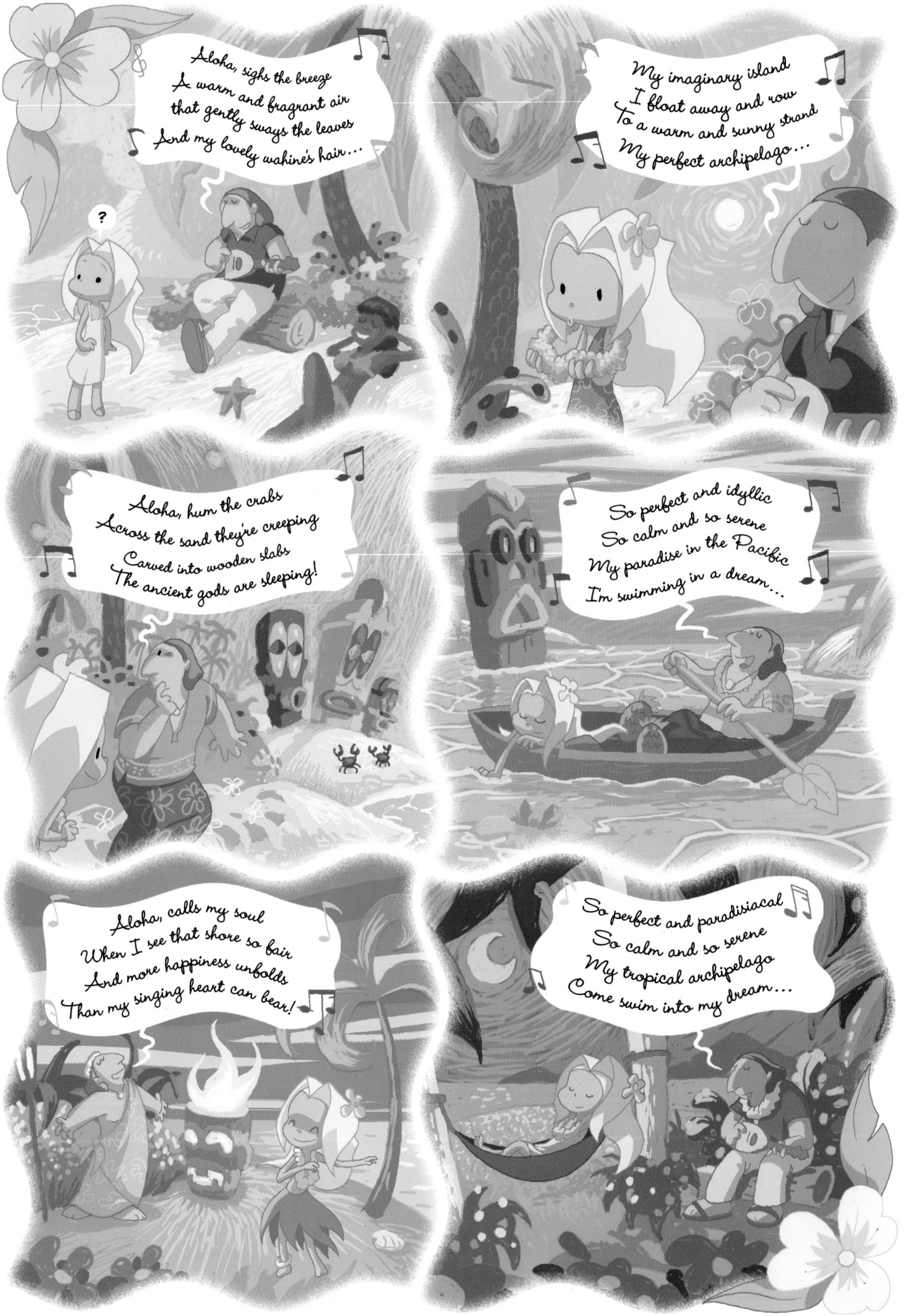
Aloha, sighs the breeze
A warm and fragrant air
that gently sways the leaves
And my lovely wahine's hair...
?
My imaginary island
I float away and row
To a warm and sunny strand
My perfect archipelago...
Aloha, hum the crabs
Across the sand they're creeping
Carved into wooden slabs
The ancient gods are sleeping!
So perfect and idyllic
So calm and so serene
My paradise in the Pacific
I'm swimming in a dream...
Aloha, calls my soul
When I see that shore so fair
And more happiness unfolds
Than my singing heart can bear!
So perfect and paradisiacal
So calm and so serene
My tropical archipelago
Come swim into my dream...

HEY, WAKE UP. WE'RE ALMOST BACK TO YOUR HOUSE.

ZᶻZMMHUH?

HIC

YOU KNOW. THERE'S SOMETHING KNEW THAT NE DAY THE NE FOR ME

BLAH. ALL THAT WINE. I'M A LIL TIPSY...

HIC

EX OBVIOUSLY, I HAVE AN PL AND I HAVE MONEY, BUT Y JST TELL ME...

OH, RIGHT. CLEM FIFFER.

WHAT'S HE BABBLING ABOUT?

AND SOMETIMES, AT MY VILLA, I HAVE XURIOUS LOTS OF MONEY AND ASH COMING F MY EARS

HEY, WHAT'S WITH THE HAND?

ANYWAY, I SAID TO MYSELF: CLEMENT FIFFER TIME AND I D THAT SERIOUS RRY...

BLEH. I DON'T UNDERSTAND A WORD HE'S SAYING...

SLEEEEEEEP...

UM...THAT'S IT...

DID...DIDJA LIKE IT?

HEH HEH...DID YOU FALL ASLEEP?

HMM?

I WAS ABOUT TO, YES...

I WAS DRIFTING OFF INTO YOUR SONG...

...ON YOUR ISLAND...

YAAWN.

SLEEP.

WHOA, IT'S LATE!

I'LL WALK YOU HOME.

VERY NICE OF YOU.

OH, WAIT... WHY'D WE COME BACK HERE?

OH, RIGHT. RATS: A SWEATER! I WAS GOING TO LEND YOU A SWEATER.

NEVER MIND, I'M FINE...

I'M ALL WARM NOW.

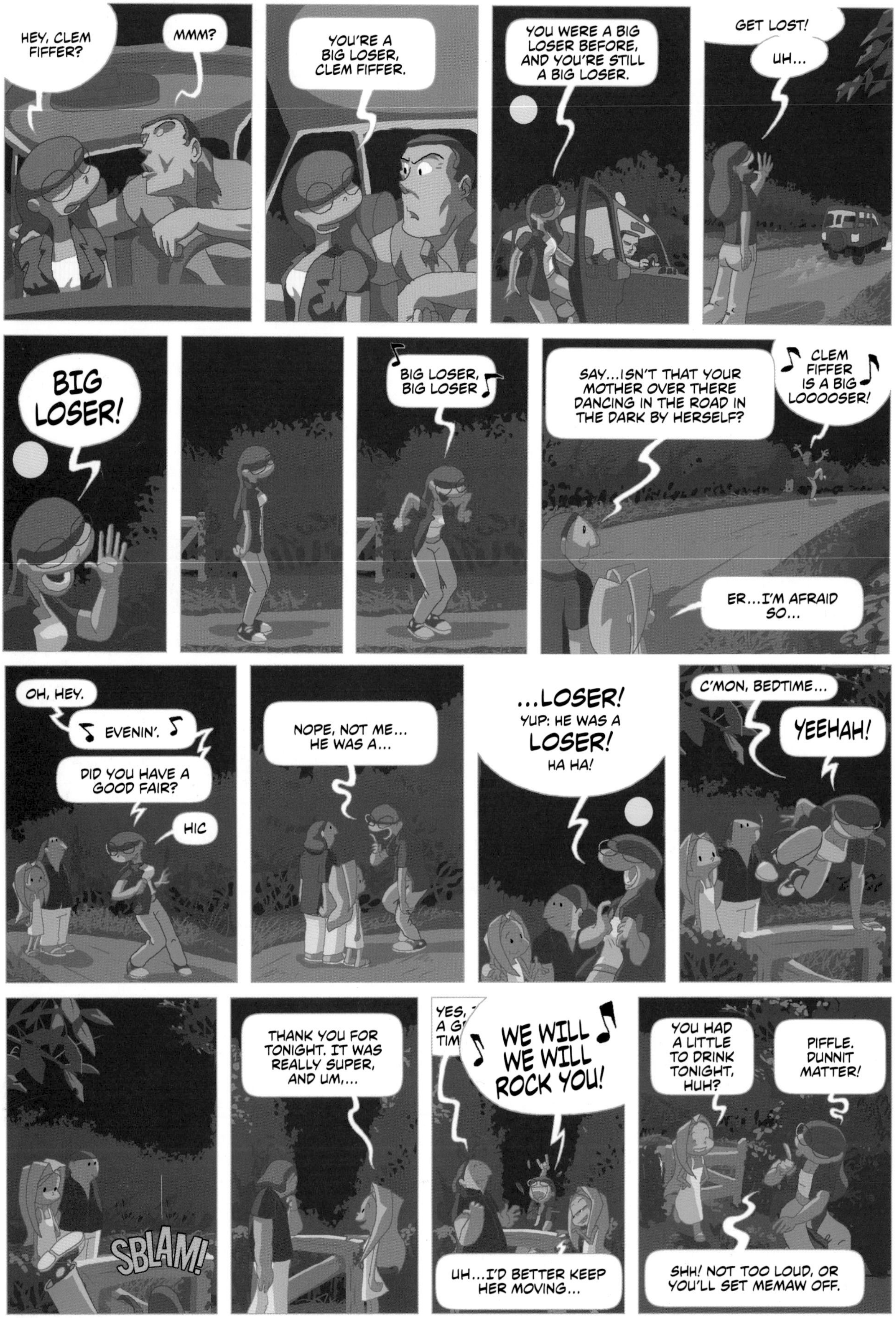
HEY, CLEM FIFFER?
MMM?
YOU'RE A BIG LOSER, CLEM FIFFER.
YOU WERE A BIG LOSER BEFORE, AND YOU'RE STILL A BIG LOSER.
GET LOST!
UH...
BIG LOSER!
BIG LOSER, BIG LOSER
SAY...ISN'T THAT YOUR MOTHER OVER THERE DANCING IN THE ROAD IN THE DARK BY HERSELF?
CLEM FIFFER IS A BIG LOOOOSER!
ER...I'M AFRAID SO...
OH, HEY.
EVENIN'.
DID YOU HAVE A GOOD FAIR?
HIC
NOPE, NOT ME... HE WAS A...
...LOSER! YUP: HE WAS A LOSER! HA HA!
C'MON, BEDTIME...
YEEHAH!
SBLAM!
THANK YOU FOR TONIGHT. IT WAS REALLY SUPER, AND UM,...
YES,
WE WILL WE WILL ROCK YOU!
UH...I'D BETTER KEEP HER MOVING...
YOU HAD A LITTLE TO DRINK TONIGHT, HUH?
PIFFLE. DUNNIT MATTER!
SHH! NOT TOO LOUD, OR YOU'LL SET MEMAW OFF.

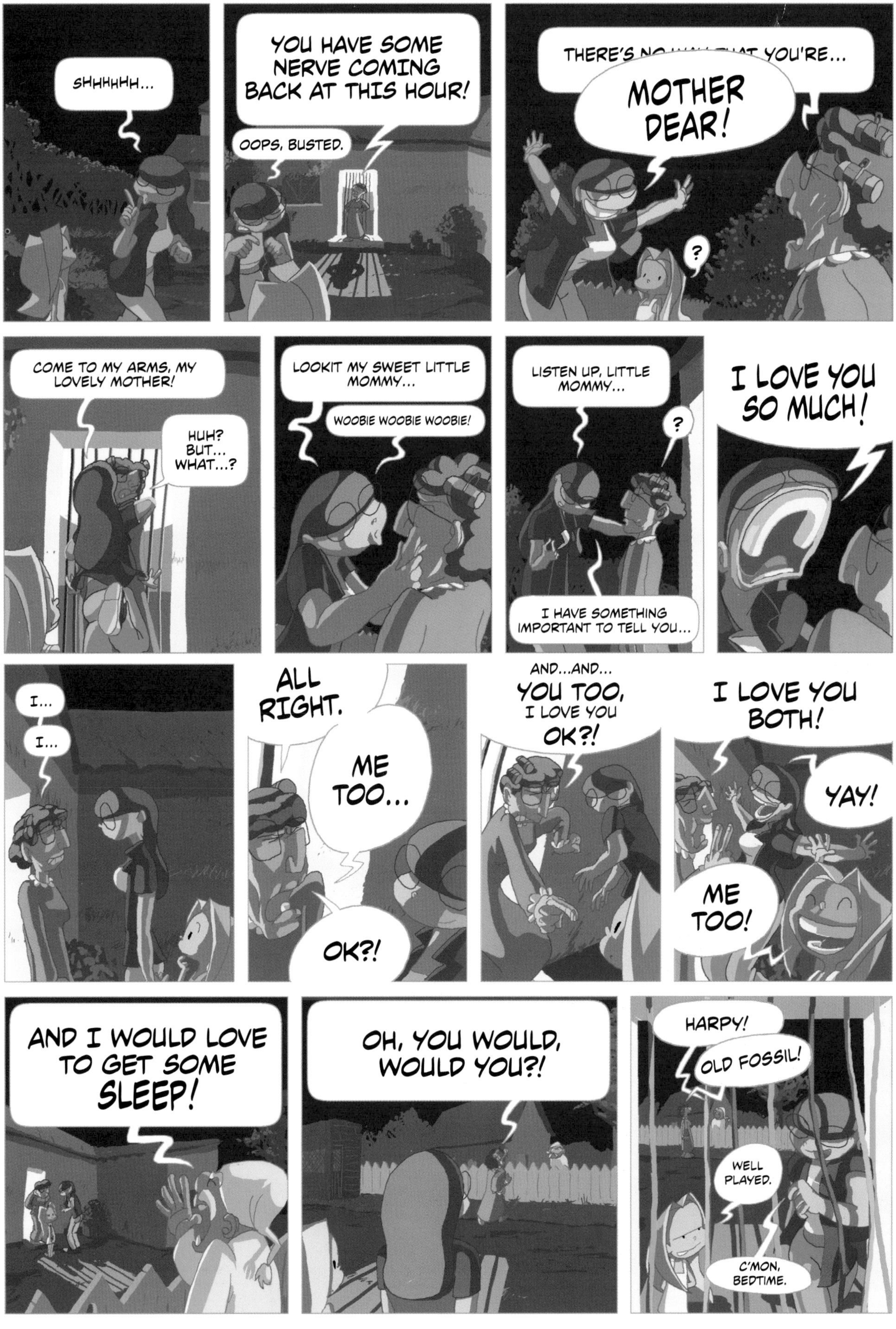
SHHHHHH...
YOU HAVE SOME NERVE COMING BACK AT THIS HOUR!
OOPS, BUSTED.
THERE'S … YOU'RE...
MOTHER DEAR!
?
COME TO MY ARMS, MY LOVELY MOTHER!
HUH? BUT... WHAT...?
LOOKIT MY SWEET LITTLE MOMMY...
WOOBIE WOOBIE WOOBIE!
LISTEN UP, LITTLE MOMMY...
?
I HAVE SOMETHING IMPORTANT TO TELL YOU...
I LOVE YOU SO MUCH!
I...
I...
ALL RIGHT.
ME TOO...
OK?!
AND...AND...
YOU TOO, I LOVE YOU OK?!
I LOVE YOU BOTH!
YAY!
ME TOO!
AND I WOULD LOVE TO GET SOME SLEEP!
OH, YOU WOULD, WOULD YOU?!
HARPY!
OLD FOSSIL!
WELL PLAYED.
C'MON, BEDTIME.

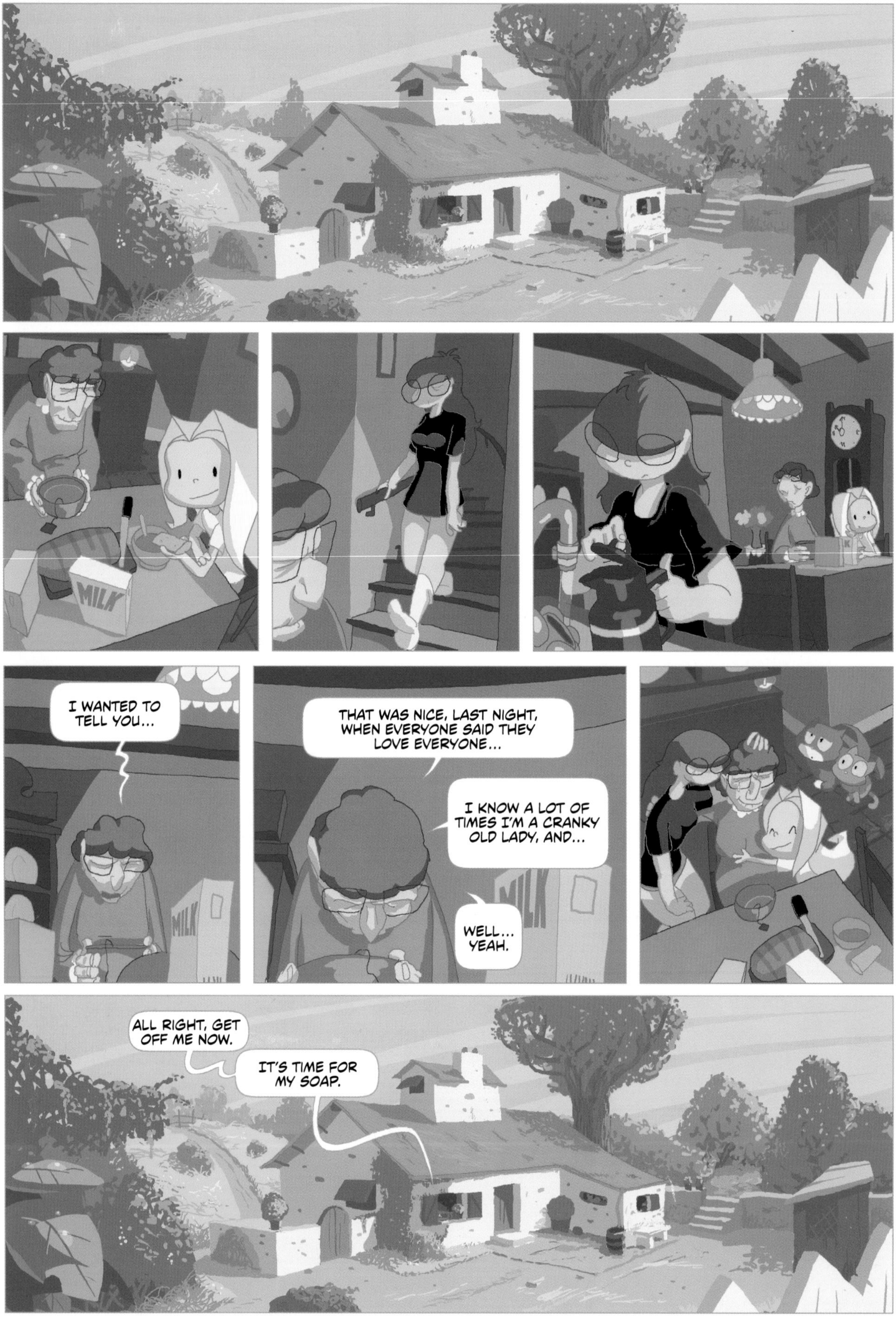
I WANTED TO TELL YOU...
THAT WAS NICE, LAST NIGHT, WHEN EVERYONE SAID THEY LOVE EVERYONE...
I KNOW A LOT OF TIMES I'M A CRANKY OLD LADY, AND...
WELL... YEAH.
ALL RIGHT, GET OFF ME NOW.
IT'S TIME FOR MY SOAP.

Exiled to the back end of a black hole, Sidera, devoured by agonizing existential questions in a cosmic crisis of laziness, decides to consult the very, very ancient keeper of knowledge…

ANCIENT KEEPER OF KNOWLEDGE, I AM, AS IT WERE, CONSUMED BY AGONIZING QUESTIONS.

EXISTENTIAL ONES.

Maybe this return to her roots and the illuminating words of wisdom from her honored ancestor will enable her to find her beloved Prince Falgor.

AH, MY DAUGHTER, REFLECT ON THIS!

WHAT KIND OF SILLY JOB IS "DEFENDER OF GALACTIC JUSTICE"?

IF YOU HAD BECOME A GALACTIC POSTAL CARRIER LIKE I TOLD YOU, YOU'D HAVE STEADY WORK AND WOULDN'T BE BOTHERING ME WITH YOUR EXISTENTIAL CRISES…

Sidera left the keeper of knowledge slightly confused…

WHAT DID SHE MEAN BY "WORTHLESS GOOD-FOR-NOTHING"?

As she wanders dazed into the countryside of Znort, she comes face-to-face with Prince Falgor…

YO.

HEY, PRINCE FALGOR!

YOU'RE HERE?!

I WAS JUST SEARCHING THE WHOLE COSMOS FOR YOU!

Exactly like in the movies, they run in slow motion in the setting suns like a couple of idiots…

Under the ultraviolet moon-glow, Sidera and the love of her life make with the smooching…

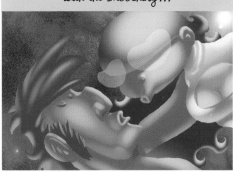

But suddenly, the image of Falgor wobbles and blurs…

SGLORG!

?

…turning into Fibfrark, the villainous polymorphic slug.

HOLY SATURN! A HOLO-COSTUME!

Quick as a flash, our heroine's foot is planted in the viscous face of the vile impostor.

BOOT!

With renewed energy, Sidera resumes her search through the galaxy to find the true Falgor…

YEHAH!

GONNA REEL HIM IN!

IT LOOKS LIKE YOUR BOOK'S REALLY MOVING ALONG…

YEAAAH!

HEH HEH HEH!

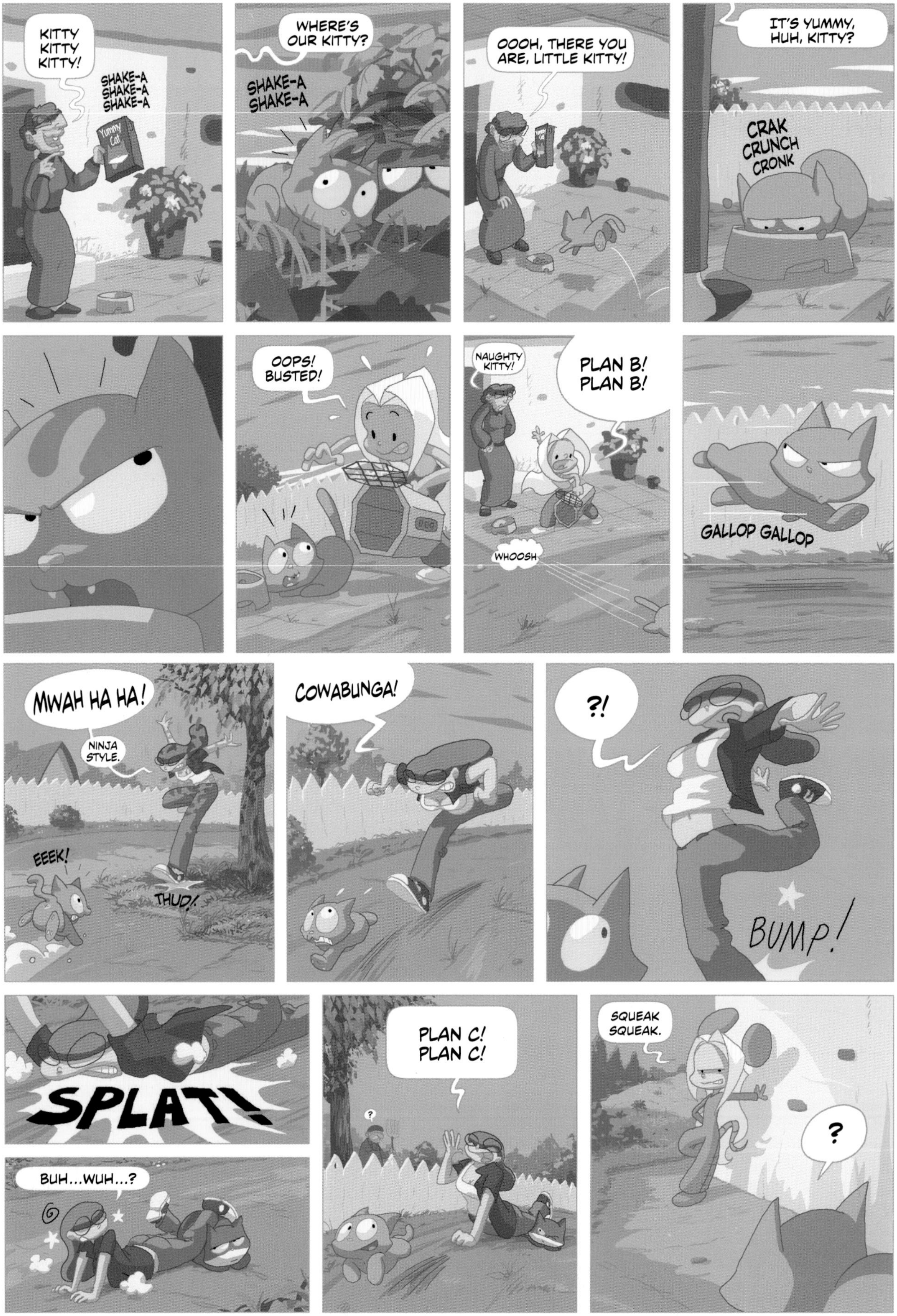
KITTY KITTY KITTY!
SHAKE-A SHAKE-A SHAKE-A
Yummy Cat
WHERE'S OUR KITTY?
SHAKE-A SHAKE-A
OOOH, THERE YOU ARE, LITTLE KITTY!
IT'S YUMMY, HUH, KITTY?
CRAK CRUNCH CRONK
OOPS! BUSTED!
NAUGHTY KITTY!
PLAN B! PLAN B!
WHOOSH
GALLOP GALLOP
MWAH HA HA!
NINJA STYLE.
EEEK!
THUD!
COWABUNGA!
?!
BUMP!
SPLAT!
BUH...WUH...?
PLAN C! PLAN C!
?
SQUEAK SQUEAK.
?

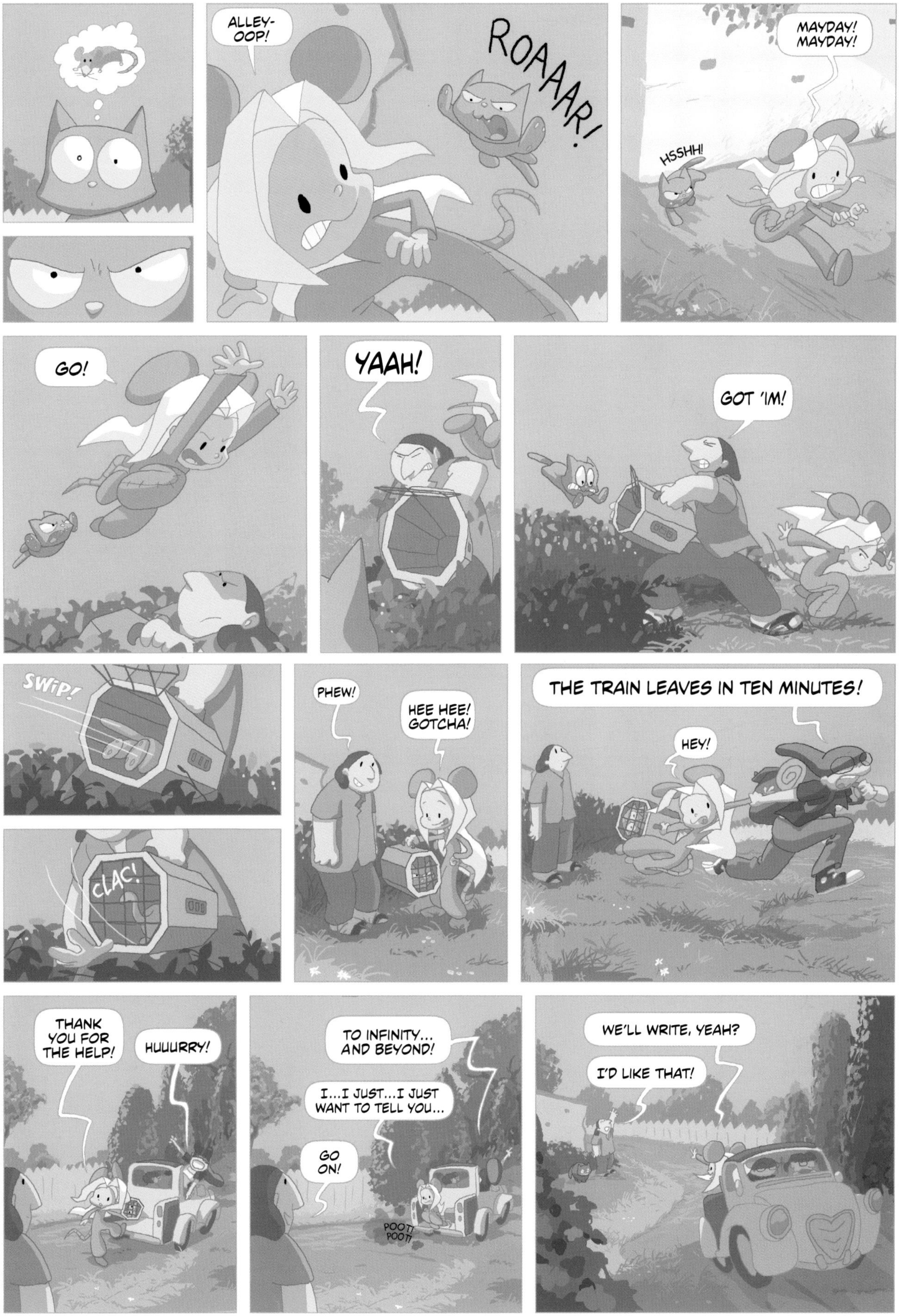
ALLEY-OOP!
ROAAAAR!
MAYDAY! MAYDAY!
HSSHH!
GO!
YAAH!
GOT 'IM!
SWIP!
CLAC!
PHEW!
HEE HEE! GOTCHA!
THE TRAIN LEAVES IN TEN MINUTES!
HEY!
THANK YOU FOR THE HELP!
HUUURRY!
TO INFINITY... AND BEYOND!
I...I JUST...I JUST WANT TO TELL YOU...
GO ON!
POOT! POOT!
WE'LL WRITE, YEAH?
I'D LIKE THAT!

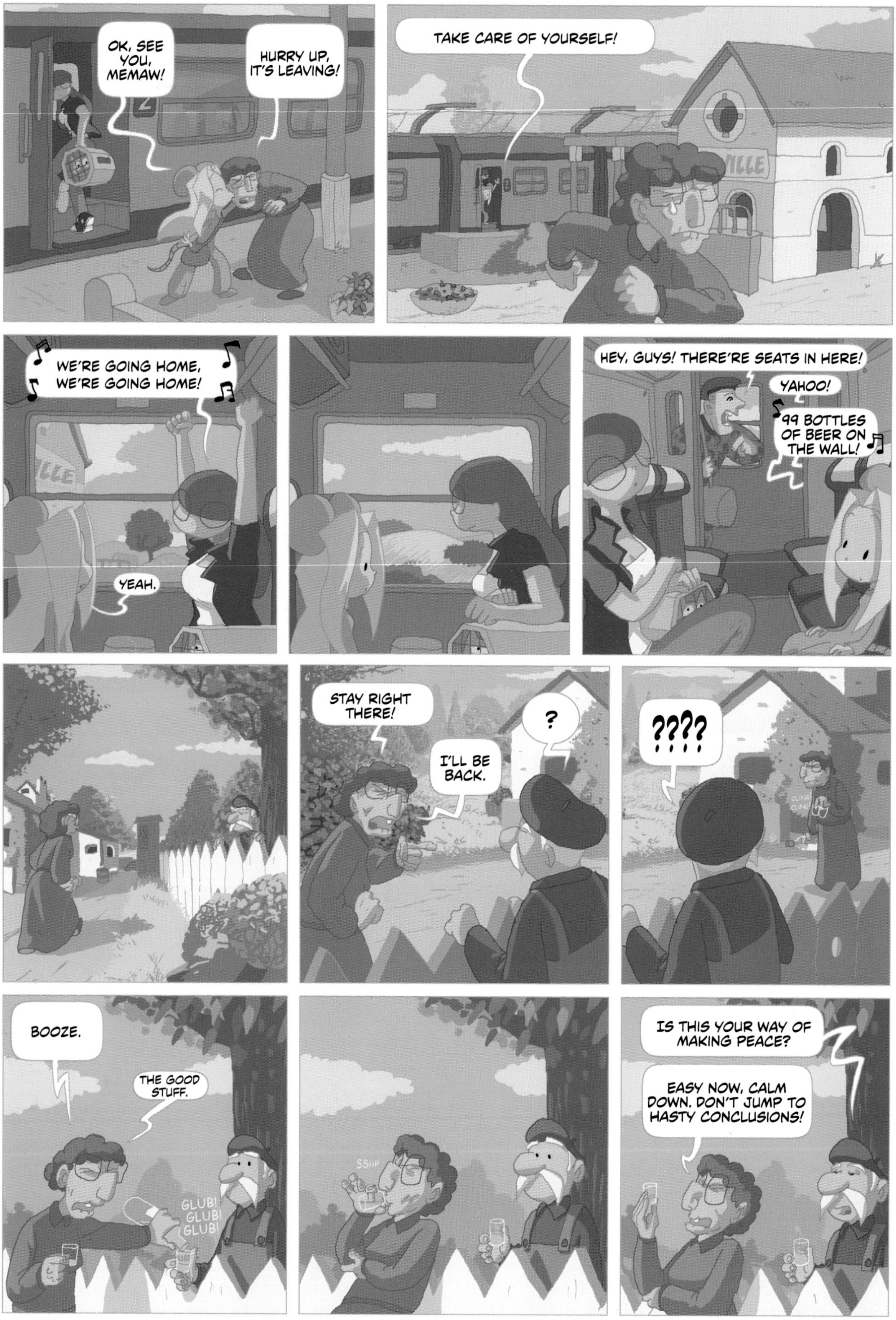
OK, SEE YOU, MEMAW!
HURRY UP, IT'S LEAVING!
TAKE CARE OF YOURSELF!
WE'RE GOING HOME, WE'RE GOING HOME!
YEAH.
HEY, GUYS! THERE'RE SEATS IN HERE!
YAHOO!
99 BOTTLES OF BEER ON THE WALL!
STAY RIGHT THERE!
I'LL BE BACK.
?
????
BOOZE.
THE GOOD STUFF.
GLUB! GLUB! GLUB!
IS THIS YOUR WAY OF MAKING PEACE?
EASY NOW, CALM DOWN. DON'T JUMP TO HASTY CONCLUSIONS!

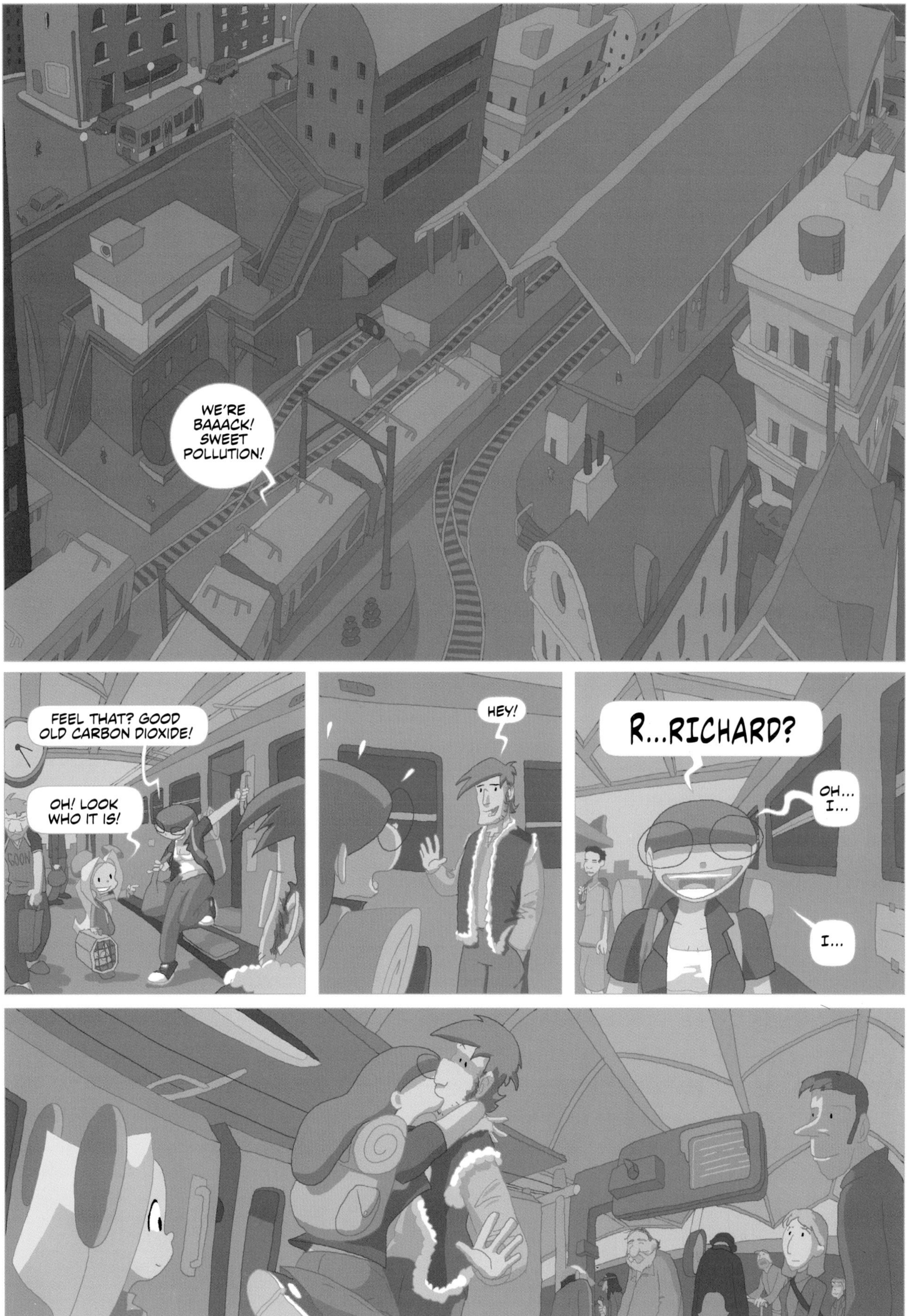
WE'RE BAAACK! SWEET POLLUTION!
FEEL THAT? GOOD OLD CARBON DIOXIDE!
OH! LOOK WHO IT IS!
GOON
HEY!
R...RICHARD?
OH... I...
I...

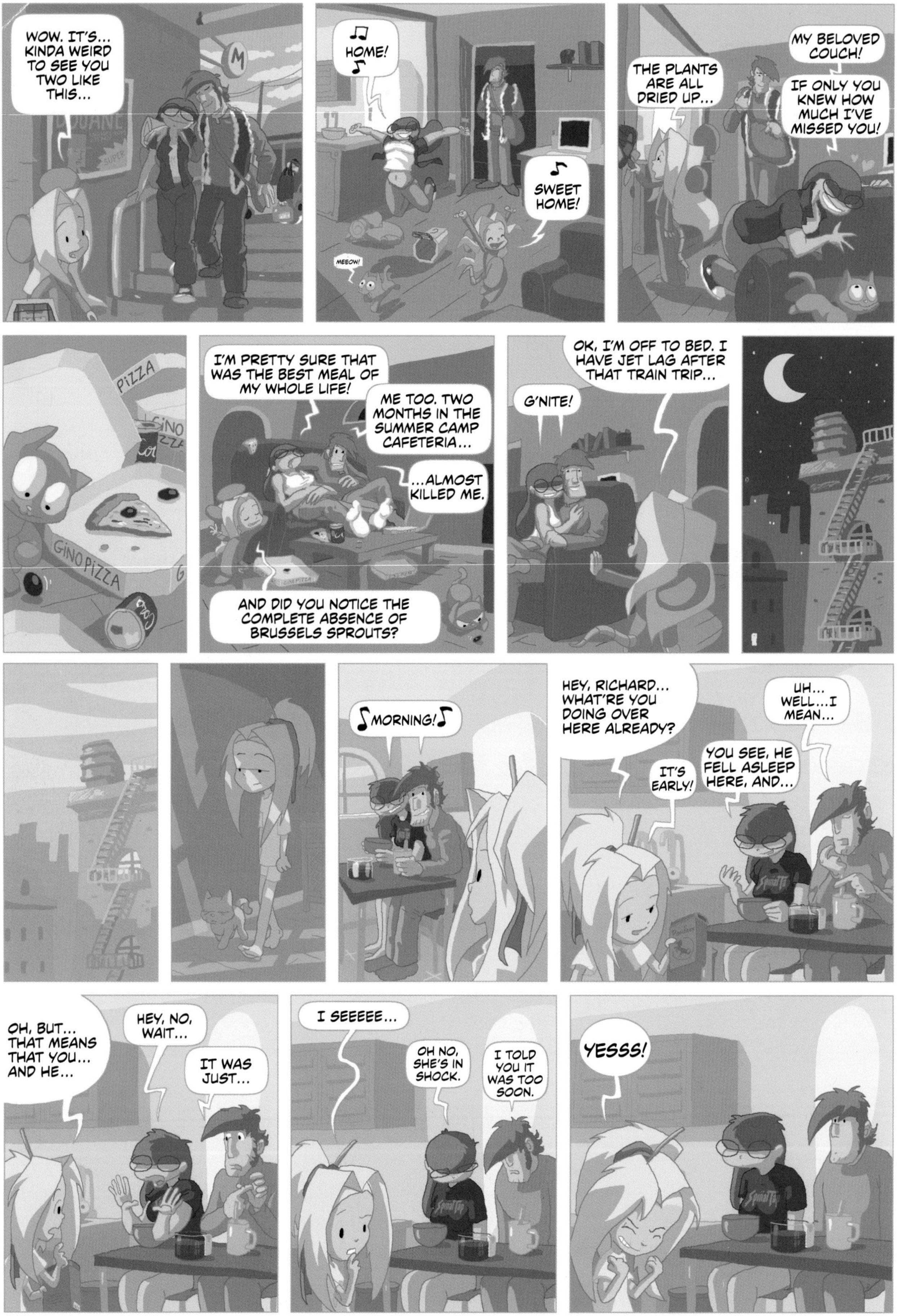

WOW. IT'S... KINDA WEIRD TO SEE YOU TWO LIKE THIS...
HOME!
SWEET HOME!
MEEOW!
THE PLANTS ARE ALL DRIED UP...
MY BELOVED COUCH!
IF ONLY YOU KNEW HOW MUCH I'VE MISSED YOU!
PIZZA
GINO PIZZA
I'M PRETTY SURE THAT WAS THE BEST MEAL OF MY WHOLE LIFE!
ME TOO. TWO MONTHS IN THE SUMMER CAMP CAFETERIA...
...ALMOST KILLED ME.
AND DID YOU NOTICE THE COMPLETE ABSENCE OF BRUSSELS SPROUTS?
OK, I'M OFF TO BED. I HAVE JET LAG AFTER THAT TRAIN TRIP...
G'NITE!
MORNING!
HEY, RICHARD... WHAT'RE YOU DOING OVER HERE ALREADY?
IT'S EARLY!
UH... WELL...I MEAN...
YOU SEE, HE FELL ASLEEP HERE, AND...
OH, BUT... THAT MEANS THAT YOU... AND HE...
HEY, NO, WAIT...
IT WAS JUST...
I SEEEEE...
OH NO, SHE'S IN SHOCK.
I TOLD YOU IT WAS TOO SOON.
YESSS!

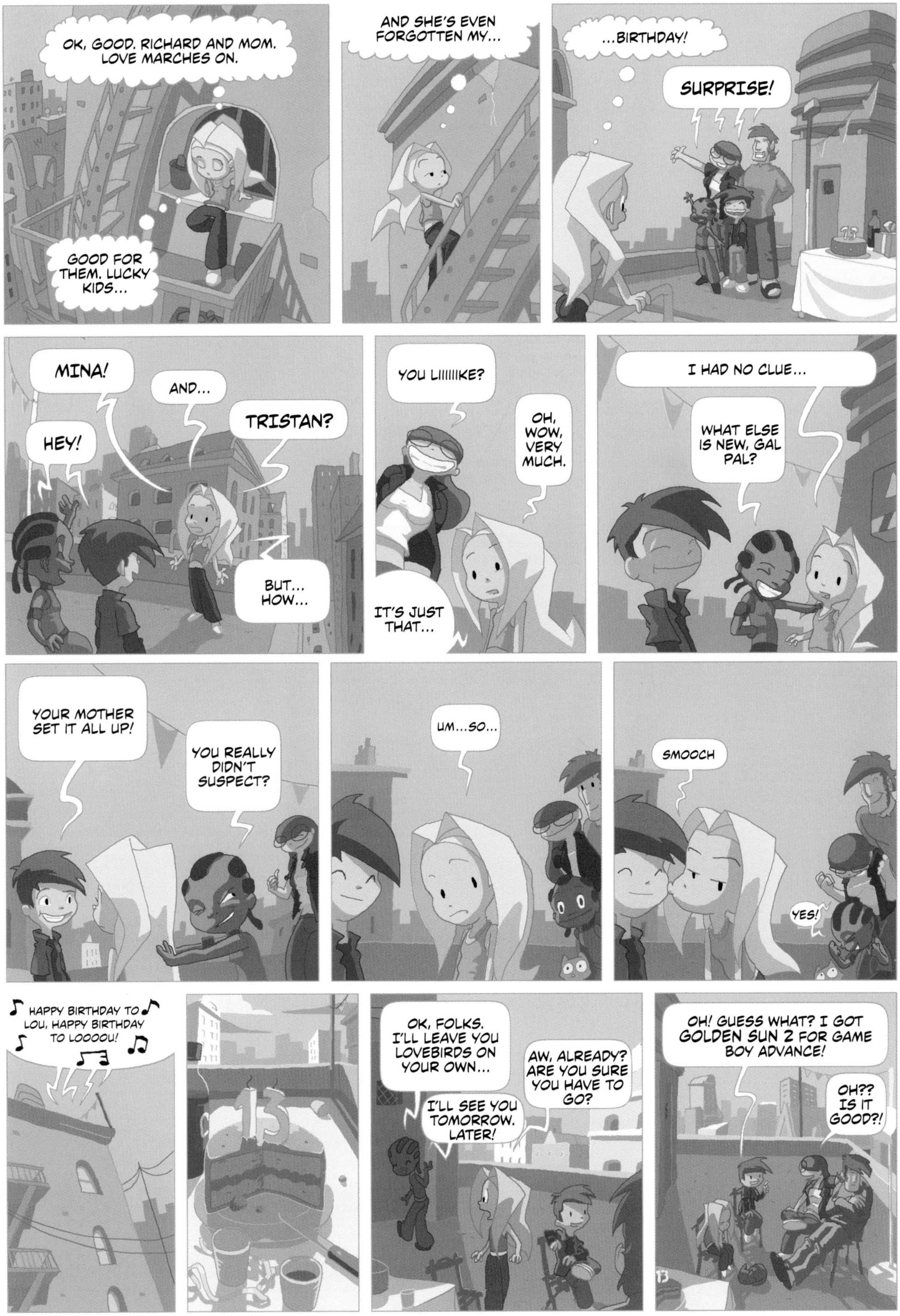
OK, GOOD. RICHARD AND MOM. LOVE MARCHES ON.
GOOD FOR THEM. LUCKY KIDS...
AND SHE'S EVEN FORGOTTEN MY...
...BIRTHDAY!
SURPRISE!
MINA!
HEY!
AND...
TRISTAN?
BUT... HOW...
YOU LIIIIIIKE?
OH, WOW, VERY MUCH.
IT'S JUST THAT...
I HAD NO CLUE...
WHAT ELSE IS NEW, GAL PAL?
YOUR MOTHER SET IT ALL UP!
YOU REALLY DIDN'T SUSPECT?
UM...SO...
SMOOCH
YES!
HAPPY BIRTHDAY TO LOU, HAPPY BIRTHDAY TO LOOOOU!
OK, FOLKS. I'LL LEAVE YOU LOVEBIRDS ON YOUR OWN...
I'LL SEE YOU TOMORROW. LATER!
AW, ALREADY? ARE YOU SURE YOU HAVE TO GO?
OH! GUESS WHAT? I GOT GOLDEN SUN 2 FOR GAME BOY ADVANCE!
OH?? IS IT GOOD?!

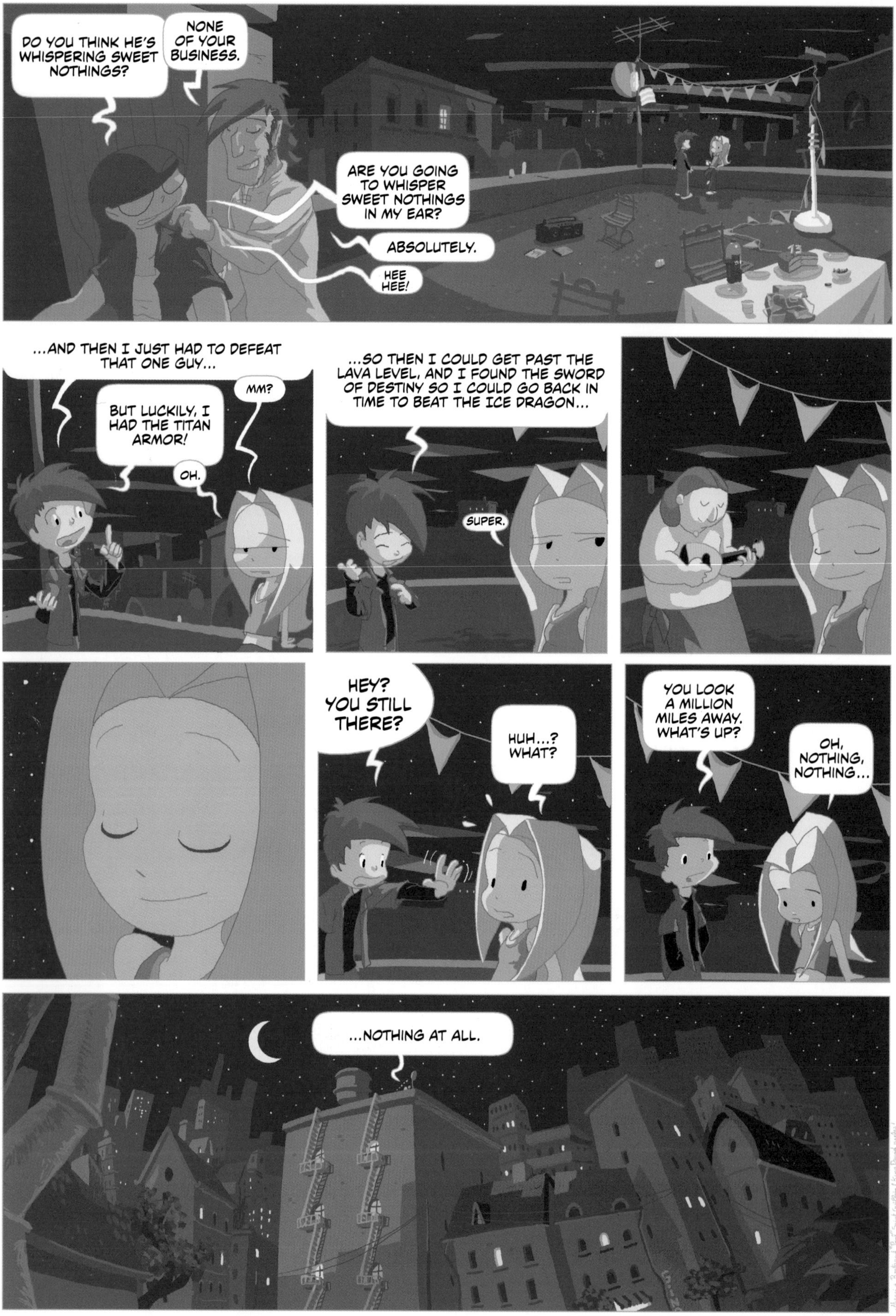
DO YOU THINK HE'S WHISPERING SWEET NOTHINGS?
NONE OF YOUR BUSINESS.
ARE YOU GOING TO WHISPER SWEET NOTHINGS IN MY EAR?
ABSOLUTELY.
HEE HEE!
...AND THEN I JUST HAD TO DEFEAT THAT ONE GUY...
MM?
BUT LUCKILY, I HAD THE TITAN ARMOR!
OH.
...SO THEN I COULD GET PAST THE LAVA LEVEL, AND I FOUND THE SWORD OF DESTINY SO I COULD GO BACK IN TIME TO BEAT THE ICE DRAGON...
SUPER.
HEY? YOU STILL THERE?
HUH...? WHAT?
YOU LOOK A MILLION MILES AWAY. WHAT'S UP?
OH, NOTHING, NOTHING...
...NOTHING AT ALL.

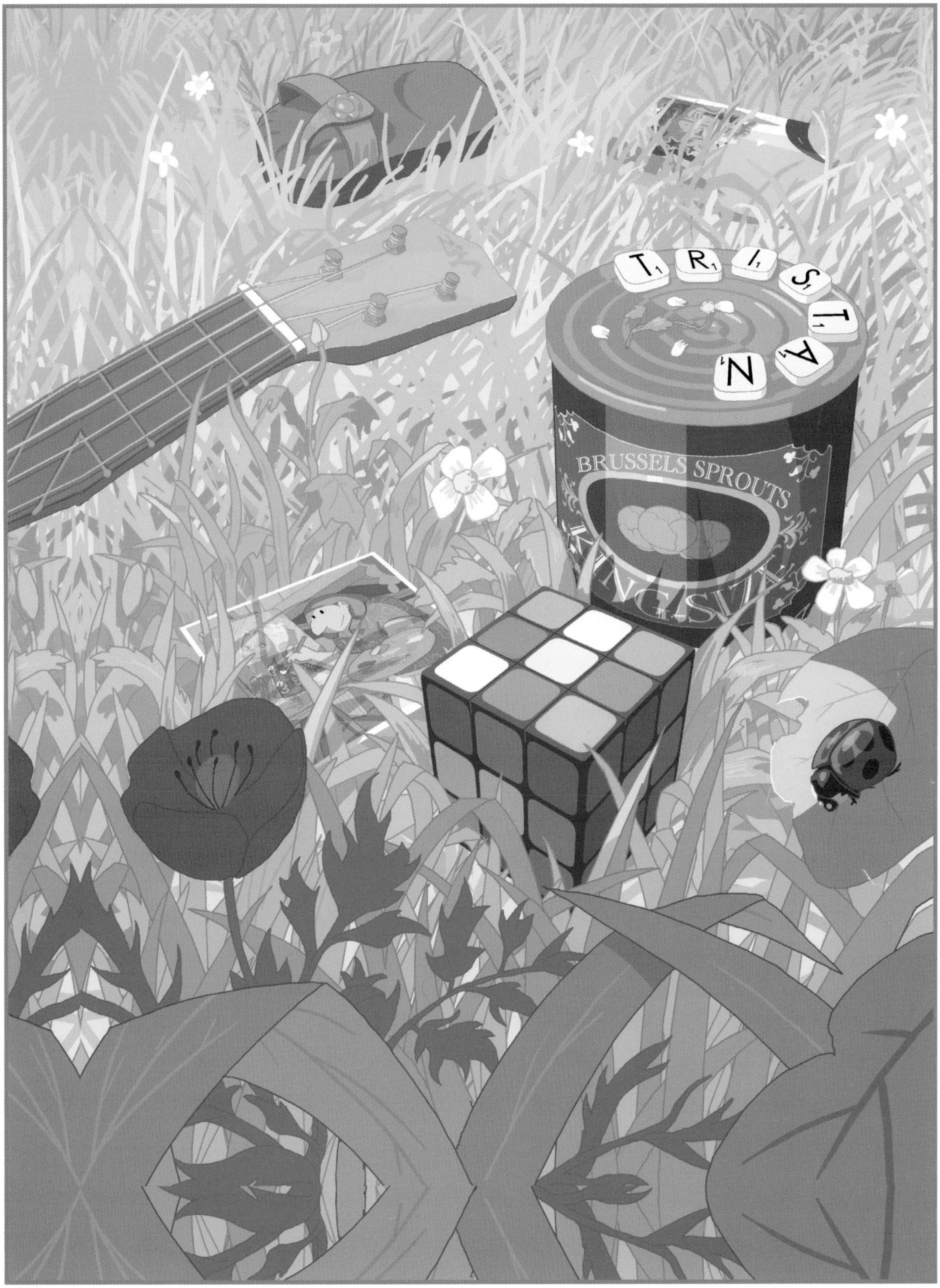
TRISTAN
BRUSSELS SPROUTS

The original back cover of the French edition

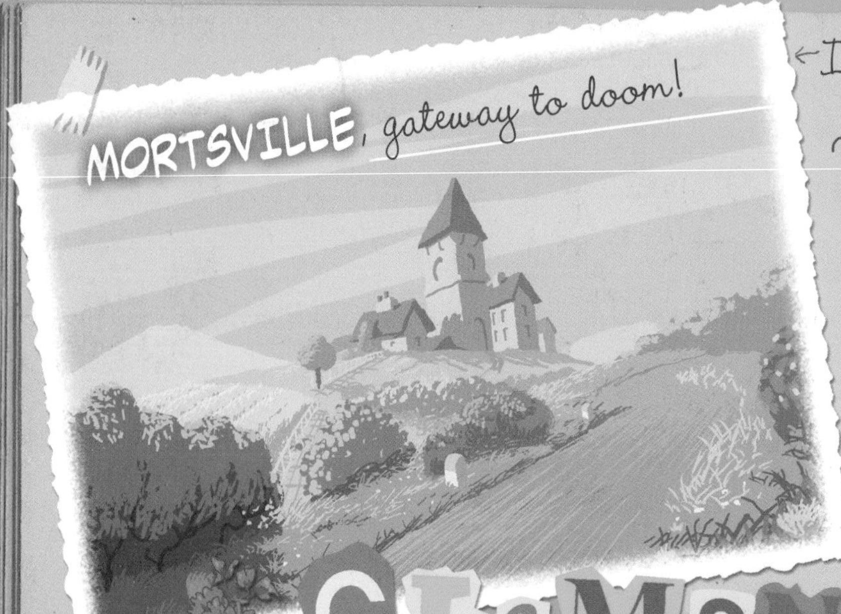
MORTSVILLE, gateway to doom!

←I exaggerate a smidge.

We are finally home. And in fact, this year, vacation went pretty well.

For example, this guy was pretty funny. ←

CLEMENT FIFFER

One of Mom's old school friends, big loser.

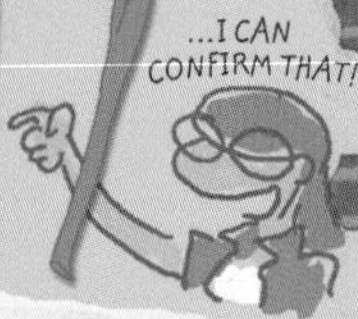
...I CAN CONFIRM THAT!

Memaw sent us this informative newspaper clipping... →

A MORTSVILLE CHAMPION!

One of our own, Clement Fiffer, swung his way to victory at the regional golf tournament, defeating the top cardiologist from the town of Fish-on-Figgle and the mayor of Moldington.

"I don't plan to stop here." our champion informed this reporter. "I intend to win big next month at the 4x4 rally over in Grim Rivers!"

Well spoken, from an athlete who has so ably filled every niche in the local sports landscape!

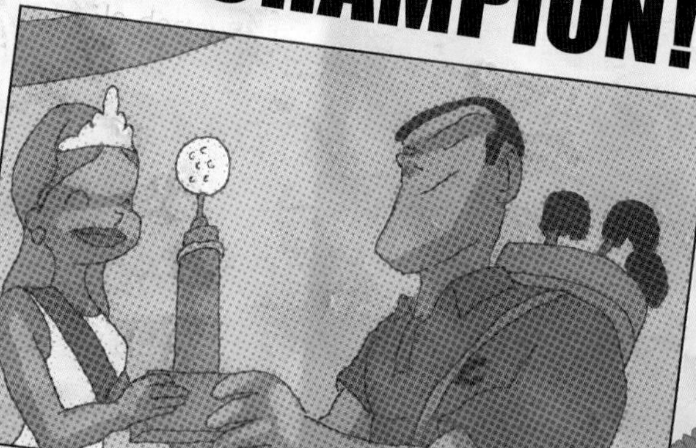
Miss Summer BBQ Festival Princess presenting the trophy to our heroic man of medicine

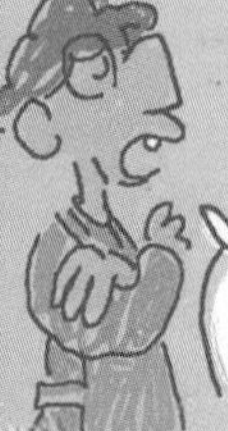
...WHAT A FINE HUMAN SPECIMEN!

Dr. Clement Fiffer, M.D.

General Practitioner

5 DeWeebe Street, Mortsville

← Never mind his business card. Anyone can see that he's a loser...

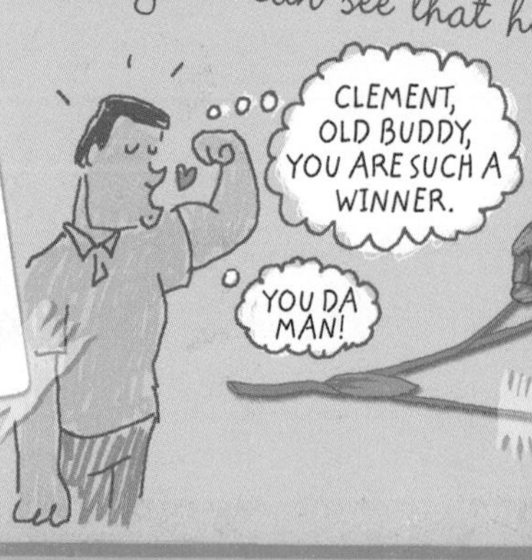
CLEMENT, OLD BUDDY, YOU ARE SUCH A WINNER.
YOU DA MAN!